VLADISLAV VANČURA
PLOUGHSHARES INTO SWORDS

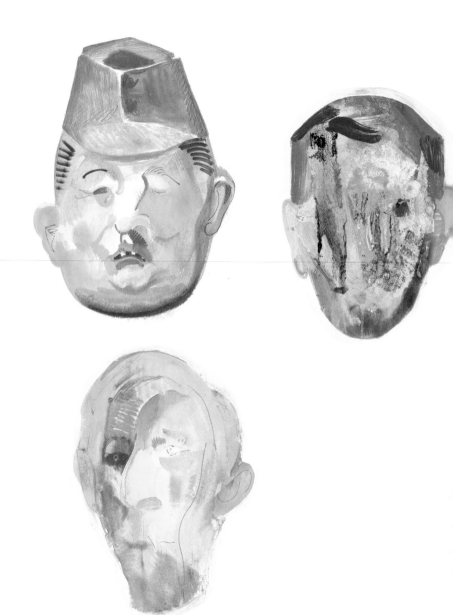

MODERN CZECH CLASSICS

Ploughshares into Swords

Vladislav Vančura

Translated from the Czech by David Short
Afterword by Rajendra A. Chitnis

Karolinum Press

KAROLINUM PRESS is a publishing department of Charles University
Ovocný trh 5/560, 116 36 Prague 1, Czech Republic
www.karolinum.cz

Pole orná a válečná was originally published in 1925, here translated
from the edition published by Naše vojsko, Prague 1966

Cover and graphic design by Zdeněk Ziegler
Edited (in part) by Robert Pynsent
Copyedited by Martin Janeček
Typeset by DTP Karolinum
Printed in the Czech Republic by Těšínské papírny, s. r. o.
First English edition

ISBN 978-80-246-4814-9 (hb)
ISBN 978-80-246-4808-8 (pdf)
ISBN 978-80-246-4810-1 (epub)
ISBN 978-80-246-4809-5 (mobi)

CONTENTS

The loam that barely covers the porphyry, gneiss and schist about the middle reaches of the River Vltava, the shallow topsoil with a smidgen of clay on the western slopes of some hills that have no name, the depths of ordinariness, the floor of destitution, is by no means so meagre for woods not to have sprung from it.

They do spring, exactly as speech – before being rendered at last by a voice – springs over the course of a long silence.

In this valley, famine has reigned for too long. The old generation of workers has sinned against itself, and health and strength have been allowed to moulder away. Pain has not been stirred to revolt beneath blows and whippings, new arrivals have become farmhands, and they have not been many. A cowed calm has been this land's clime, and passion its only lightning flash.

The workers' wages, counted out into the palms of their hands, are paltry, paltry is their life, and paltry are the episodes of their despair. Tales told lack all edge and a word can scarcely elevate truth, when its ordinariness is general and of no greater value than dust and ashes.

A landscape threaded by a river, a landscape with bare rocks, with tiny fields stretching in narrow strips across the sides of hillocks, with a church standing above water, stabbing the pool with the reflection of its cross, a landscape both poor and beautiful, tufted with bushes, sunk in lamentation and pathos, enclosed to the north, the south, the east and the west by distance.

The barrier of its destitution is open space.

The world may be vast, but somewhere it ends, and the cartographer has marked the spot:

"Hic sunt leones."

And so the globe is no greater than the shadow cast by the tree of knowledge, a shadow haunted by a dark legend. This cramped spot is the world in which events in the life of Ouhrov manor are told.

During winters of indigence that inspire anger, in the evening after the stars have come out, at hours of death, in seasons of love and during bouts of insanity fired by liquor, this dark corner opens a chink and you can see roads leading into the distance, lined with crosses to terrify anyone who dares try to escape. Female saints glare at his neck as he passes by the trees on which suicides have hung; he'll be happy enough to turn back, the roads being fit only for carts that creak and seesaw over the uneven surface, and Ouhrov breeds none but ox handlers, ploughboys and wagoners to serve its estate.

In this confine, in this abeyance of life, dwelleth naught but passion and death.

Seven tumps break up the landscape, and that superstitious number holds sway in these parts. A horse walks alongside its flailing shaft, the axle-tree creaks and the cursing never lets up. It does not have far to go, and the sameness and repetition drag on along the tracks.

Too much blather has gone on pastures and the girded sower, to no effect has the ploughman's labour been extolled. No one teeters on the brink of precipices, no one seeds the fields, or works a share plough, and the words used by silly singers have been long forgotten. 'Tis unspeakable how the farm labourer has been made the butt of adage, accorded names that reek of sentimentality.

The fellows who do this kind of work are vulgar and coarse, pig-headed or shiftless, but also capable of working till they drop. They fornicate and they get drunk.

The five-beam motorised plough now carves up the land and no ploughman needs put his weight behind the stilts of a plough drawn by oxen. The sickle and the scythe are almost forgotten.

The summer days of 1913 had passed and the fingertips of autumn were heralding the wind about to blow across the stubble fields and the cold to follow. The harvest had been piled into ricks, the days had begun to shorten and a merciful Saturday, summing up the working week, was about to hand out the beggarly wages. Small they might be, but the pub is nearby and is not a large one.

The estate managers Saček and Chot, two monsters deserving of a measure of compassion, prone to exaggerate their importance, were now, grubby notebook and tally in hand, exercising their authority amid the scrawny gang.

A foundling, Řeka, a halfwit bent low with shame and centuries-old contempt, one whose name – meaning 'river' – is pure accident or a bit of bureaucratic lyricising devised by some dreary jackass when the foundling's guardian wanted to have him called something different from his own František..., the sun-scorched Řeka was becoming a man of substance as he counted his five florins. His due having been received, his perspective closed down and he awoke to a new world.

"Along with you," Hora told him, "what are you waiting for?"

Some lame words made to rise to his tongue, but he offered no reply and his insatiable thought severed itself from the lengthy process of speaking. He turned, getting even more in the way of the others, and, at the same spot, planting his clogs where Řeka's feet had been, a large man took up position.

This labourer's money did not sound right and he re-counted it from closed fist to palm, not dropping it from any great height, and muttering one number after another. His eyes lacked the resplendence of evening that was falling upon them, and if he had turned towards the manor house or the shallow prism shape of the pub, on which the roof, too narrow, had been set awry, he would not even have seen things so close at hand. He wanted no more, nor could he do more, than to persist in doing his sums.

Another man was approaching the seat of judgement by money, laughing loud and gesturing wildly. One man leaned on another for support, ignorant of the difference between work time and pay time. The wives of these drunkards rolled their eyes and between one heartbeat and the next uttered a word of abuse.

Two old men stepped out of the huddle and headed past the sheds full of implements and the weighbridge towards the trough that was the animals' water hole.

Hora and Ber they were, two widowers who, like a thing that creepeth upon the earth and a piece of tinder, recalled the difference between a sneaky creature and a paltry, lifeless object only willed into motion by a playful God; Hora's arms, bearded like barley, hung by his sides and he dragged one leg behind him, there being no cure for its impairment.

"The security of old age, insurance and all the other nonsense they come out with," he said, not mincing his words either, "I'd sell the lot for the bushel of rye they might give me each autumn. Where's the certainty they promise me? Being poor means having to do what others tell you, and old age is nothing but biding your time."

Ber replied, smashing one fist into the palm of his other hand: "It could be that among the paperwork and stuff taken down by officials there is a record of your infirmity and you could be home and dry, since there are hospices and poorhouses where there's nothing to do bar a bit of cleaning and tidying."

"Seven times," said Hora, "seven times I've seen the inside of institutions like that and everyone had striped jackets, sticks and some sort of coupons. When the bell rang in the middle of the building, they went to be fed and then waited again, then ate again next time the signal came."

This talk of the sick man's hopes dragged on for a long time until, finally, Ber brought it to a patronising close like someone in charge of the destinies of such poor wretches: "Dream on, be as keen as you like on the idea, you flea-ridden sod, and even if you got in, they'd soon boot you out again, you and all your bugs and the scabies that gives you that tingling!"

Meanwhile the two old boys had been joined by a herdsman, who, having nothing to contribute, just snuffled and sighed.

"Well," he opined, "before you know it, maybe even tomorrow, the rains will be upon us. I'm pretty sure we'll see a turn for the worse."

By way of response Hora looked back at the farmyard, now deserted. Five women were just leaving by the gate; it was approaching seven. The manor house had veiled its hideousness in the dusk, the trough and puddles glinted and all talk was fading away. Days at Ouhrov ended quietly. Night did nothing to deaden the pain, but it did muffle its voice.

František Hora was seventy-two and he had spent that entire lifetime in the fields of the Ouhrov estate, in its stables and cowsheds and out in the great yard. He had no particular likes, nor any grievous sins. He was neither poacher nor thief and the drabness that was his suit lent him some value, for as long as he was fit.

There had been that time when, with much shouting and whooping, he had decked his hat with a posy of wild flowers and, no less tipsy than the others, answered the call-up. An accordion, scintillating like an acoustic torch, had led them to the county town.

"Don't go asking questions," they told Hora when he faltered in his merriment. "Ask no questions and stop worrying. The demands of the army are clear and you'll soon get the hang of it. For the next three years, František, you won't see any cattle, so keep singing and be off with you."

The three stations on the way were called the first, second and third years of service. A hayrack, which the publican had set up outside even before daylight, jangled with a primitive array of glass, artificial flowers and grasses dyed as gaudy as the devil's broom. Peasants' horses were at the manger, turning their lovely eyes towards František, who, knowing his place even in his cups, was standing beside them. He unhitched the traces and having fashioned some loops, tossed them two by two over the wheelers' flanks. He tugged at their saddle pads and made everything neat and tidy.

Before handsome young peasants are brought into line by the demands of army life, they sit around in taprooms and drink to their heart's content. This time, bottles passed from mouth to mouth and tankards swung up and down like a balance beam with a stuffed purse on one pan and the measly mite of a working man on the other. Like clockwork, like hammer on anvil, drunkenness struck the oak table top.

Let's go for it! Mustn't waste a single drop, drink on, my thirsty lieutenant, drink till your brain gives up. Pull the string! And down the hatch! The one who drank died – but so did the one who didn't. Sound the beer-mug trumpet! Doesn't a drunk man have a candle inside his head? Right then, make yourself scarce if you've had your fill so you don't go and snuff it out.

"Hey!" one old gannet bellowed, after thumping the window frame with his fist. "Come on, František, the sky never quenched anyone's thirst, come inside, get drinking and face the recruitment board with a skinful. Get pissed to pieces, you're not the one paying!"

Hora raised the brimming glass of brandy and didn't hold back, for this moment could earn him some renown and esteem on the Ouhrov estate.

An image of the pub's interior glinted on the curved surface of the glass, taking in the landlord's doxy and the figure of the mayor, who appeared more elongated than potbellied. Hora drank on and both image and brandy diminished until finally the empty glass enveloped the drinker's nose like the bell cloches gardeners use to protect young asparagus shoots.

When it was time to leave, the recruits came out and the farmers, having finished off their own pints, harnessed their horses. They took their time, but they still arrived before those on foot reached the outskirts of the town of Hradec. However, František Hora need not have got out of bed that day. He staggered over to a poplar tree by the roadside and there he lost his balance and fell into the ditch. The local constable, guardian of the parish peace, who was literally meant to be the poor man's guardian angel, vented his anger by giving his man a solid thump, thereby bringing relief to his stomach: František turned his entrails inside out, with no regard for keeping the place clean, tidy and quiet.

This incident did not go unpunished, though it did become the most famous thing the stablehand ever did, because his infirmities meant that he could not even do his military service. Since the threshold of infancy, since as far back as he could remember, nothing, no single moment had been greater, for he was so drunk that the sea of the world came right up to his knees. No one could ever consume the lakes of brandy that he swallowed that day, for with the passage of time everything grows, enlarged by the remembrance of them.

The stablehand's marriage had been a simple and sudden affair. About forty years previously, one long-forgotten winter or summer's day, a young maid was taken on at Ouhrov manor to feed the horses and do the mucking-out. At the time, František's plank bed stood in the west-facing angle of the stable, in a nook adorned by cobwebs and swallows' nests. The new arrival was anything but pretty and her tattered green skirt did her no favours.

The estate manager, having opened the cutting shed, pointed his stick towards a small heap of straw and said: "That's where you'll be sleeping." However, after he had gone, she grabbed it and carried it to the stables.

"Here I am and here I'll stay," she said, "if you're freezing cold in the night, come to me. Luckily, I've got plenty of everything."

After she had put out her lamp. František did not hesitate, but waving his arms about spookily in the dark, tried to find her, groping at the damp walls with quivering hand. He took her and they made love to the snorting of horses.

"My name's Anna," she said and František said in reply: "I'll buy you a shawl covered in flowers and with tassels dangling like fingers at the end of an arm."

Five months later, the fodder girl became pregnant, which the other women found funny: "Who on earth put the tuck in that green skirt of yours, making it so short?"

"You're right," she replied, "we've been very thorough." She was to have a brief weep that evening, but she would soon cheer up again.

Even then František Hora did not have much to say. For three months he set aside one florin, then with the money wrapped safe in his motley scarf, he set off to see the priest at Smrdov.

"We're a twosome," he said as he entered the clergyman's abode, "who wish to enter into wedlock – that's me, a farm worker, name of Hora, and Anna Myslbeková."

"All right," the peasant cleric replied, "so where's the bride-to-be?"

"She's pregnant," said Hora, looking about him as if looking for her. The rectory was not shaken to its foundations, nor did the priest cross himself.

"Come on in," he said, holding the door open with his rough hand.

"This book contains all the exhortations, advice and instructions that relate to marriage. Come back with Anna and I will read it to you to make you aware of them."

Five times they heard the priest speaking the language of books without understanding anything but the parable of the mustard seed, the tale of what befell the prodigal son – for whom they felt sorry, and the talk of miracles, alas, all too divine. The priest himself could not confirm that any of these things were essential to a wedding.

Anna's belly kept expanding at a rate disproportionate to their expanding knowledge of religion and they would go home from these sessions like those who, at school, had to put up with the waffling of the reverend catechist, and meanwhile they were falling behind with their work.

Thrice did František's name descend from the pulpit, thrice was it announced to the dearly beloved in the congregation and no one said a word, for the pointlessness of the ritual was beyond all doubt.

When the wedding day came, František mucked out the stables and entered the byre with the words: "I'm ready." He had to give Anna a quick hand because she was behind with her work, then off they went.

Before they reached Smrdov, František slipped the pack, prepared the night before, off his shoulder and they put on their shoes, he fixed his collar while Anna wrapped herself in her shawl and slipped her tunic from her shoulders. They entered the gaping void of the church and followed the service listless and with the humility that Churches deem a virtue. Finally, they knelt and saw the priest saying the words.

Insofar as a rite can be solemn, this wedding was that. Words filled the expanse of the church right up to the vaulted ceiling and the rafters painted all over with stars. The priest turned away from the altar, as a reaper turns to face the vastness of his field, and Anna and František uttered the words: "I do take thee without duress, freely and wholeheartedly."

They made their way back, again barefoot, and barefoot they toiled until the birth.

Married workers were meant to be accommodated in a long, shingle-roofed hut. Eleven doors and another eleven opened onto the road and onto the yard, but the two estate managers had their quarters at the end and by the gate. Narrow passageways, ending in storerooms, gave access to the two rows of dwellings, and each room had just one window. František, as he proceeded from one to the next, sized up all those hollow prisms. Damp and the tracery drawn by the rain that had come in through the now decrepit roof had left their same mark on all of them. Here a blackened corner marked the spot where a stove had once stood, there a missing paving slab, or a plank that had come adrift, had left gaping holes in which rats squealed. František did not possess even a table, and so, having pondered on his penury, he declined the rooms that he was being offered.

"We'll each give Potměšil a florin so they'll let us cook in our own pots. Two florins is a decent sum and Potměšil will be glad of them because he likes his tipple and he's penniless."

And so it came about. They made pallets from sacks and horse blankets and, having stuffed them, carried them to their new home.

For six days they got on, for six nights the Horas slept on their own beds and peace reigned. However, discord soon descended and Potměšil, almost sober, took some chalk and drew a border between Hora's patch and his own. Having marked out a right-angled triangle, whose hypotenuse went from the stove to the middle of the door, he said:

"This part is where you'll live."

"All right," František replied. "It's less than I've paid for, but I'm not going to argue."

Meanwhile, the pregnant Anna's time was coming closer and all minds were on the birth. Mrs Potměšil ripped up a duvet cover to make plenty of nappies, furious at being forced so to dissipate her property.

At about seven one Friday evening, Anna Myslbeková began having pains, which came back at ever shorter intervals, and, knowing that her time had come, she rose to go. Her sheaf of straw still lay in the middle of the cowshed.

"I haven't finished my work," she told the womenfolk, "and night's caught up with me. Go and tell František to fetch the midwife."

They did as bidden and František made haste.

Having crossed the yard, Anna entered the Potměšil room and dropped into her corner. Time oscillated hither and yon. The voice of pain grew louder and the din of the moment rose higher and higher like the smoke of a bonfire or the call of hospitals.

The midwife, who also nursed the sick and washed the dead, acclaimed accessory of death and of life in the making, got everything ready for bathing the new baby, sure in her mind that Anna was going to have a boy. Mrs Potměšil took a sheet from her chest, and although twilight had not yet fallen, she lit the lamp. They chatted and time slipped past the mother-to-be's corner.

Eleven struck and František came back to ask what was what.

"Nothing yet," they replied, "you go and sleep in the stable, you and Potměšil."

Around five in the morning, act two of the birth, the birth itself, began.

"Don't be afraid, Anna, don't be afraid," the midwife said, "it's going to be all right," then she stopped mid-utterance, suddenly scared as she touched the four fingers of the baby hand that had slipped out.

"This abnormality means a transverse lie and spells trouble. Go and hitch up the horses and get her to the hospital in Hradec."

Outside, day had begun to dawn. The cowherds rose from their beds and set about their statutory labours.

"Tchah!" they said in reply to František, "Why all the fuss, doesn't every woman giving birth get pains?"

František could not take his fears with him to the steward's room and bellow into the sleeper's ear. It was too early. He went back and waited two hours without anything happening. The pains had passed and the mother was dozing. Something of the serenity and repose of death entered the dwelling and a chance silence fell amid the voices of morning. It was striking seven when Anna's hand moved.

The death of working folk echoes to hammer blows and the ring of scythes. It had never entered the Ouhrov estate so slowly and silently, though now they recognised it for what it was. It was coming, getting nearer, raining and snowing oblivion.

František dashed out to prepare the horses and in no time was standing outside the hut. One last time the midwife put her temple to Anna's swollen belly, listening to the foetus's sounds with a wild and futile joy.

"It's alive," she cried, "get there as fast as you can!"

They picked up Anna's body and placed it on the wagon. František yanked the horses round towards the road and the wagon hurtled without stopping as far as the village of Trnová, where the doctor lived.

In the depths of the man's fear a new hope had begun to rise.

"Whoa!" he shouted and before the wagon had even stopped he hurled himself at the doorbell.

"Go back home, she's been dead over an hour," the doctor said.

But František did not turn the horses round. He listened to the clatter of the cart, the thudding of hooves and the clangour of their shoes. He could but infuse the track with weeping and bewail the corpses alone. Unhurried, the horses arrived outside the hospital, where František heard the selfsame assurance: She's dead.

This crazy certainty quite deadened his spirit. He waited, emotionless and silent, while Anna lay in the hospital mortuary.

An autopsy was carried out the following day. Her belly was cut open from womb to liver to reveal a gleaming blood clot, covered by the peritoneum. All this matter having been lifted away, the foetus's tiny hand appeared, with the umbilical cord wound round it. A small amount of blood trickled from the external genitalia. The uterus yawned through the terrible opening with the placenta and amnion projecting from it. The main body of the womb was empty. The foetus was lodged in the cervix in a simple rectal position with its head lying, roughly speaking, between its legs and its left arm. The right arm, pressed back towards the sacrum, was red and swollen.

In his report, the medical examiner stated that the cause of death was abdominal shock caused by incomplete rupturing of the uterus.

František Hora returned home the following day and, having abandoned the horses in the middle of yard, he hastily set about selling all that he possessed. This produced five florins and another five florins were paid him as an advance on his wages. He used the money to bury Anna Myslbeková in a pauper's grave.

Thereafter, Hora lived thirty years up to the day that struck another blow. Hunger and satiety, work and rest, falsehood and truth, all this came turn and turn about as the days passed by, and František could not tell the difference. He drove his horses, daydreamed and grew old.

Once, after Hora had become frail and decrepit, a young horse caught him on a knee joint with a shoe nail. They had been working in the forest; it was snowing, evening was drawing on and the other workmen had already left. Hora did not start moaning. He snapped a branch and made himself a crutch, then he dragged himself over to the tree trunks bearing down on the wagon's axles. He got up and fell again, not even feeling much pain, until he finally sat sideways on the logs and, careless as to where the boisterous horses might take him, he cracked his whip. The animals calmed down and made their way at a walking pace all the way back to the gateway to the grange. Henceforth Hora was a cripple, and his wounds refused to heal. He couldn't walk beside horses, he couldn't lever a shovel, he couldn't lift a sheaf on a pitchfork. He became an animal feeder and waited for death.

Many years previously, before he met Anna Myslbeková, František had carted to Hradec a gift sent by the great landowner of Ouhrov for the city's poor.

The Baron's good works were on a grand scale. The poor of the manor would have gobbled in an instant more than he gave away in a year, for on this estate they had gone hungry for nine generations. He could put on a banquet for them every day, without giving them any more than their due, and he expected them to be grateful. Paying good wages is good business, but Baron Danowitz was niggardly in such matters, as befits an aristocrat. He worked his day labourers hard while supporting imbecilic art projects, the fatherland, gambling dens, whores and, now and again, the Hradec poorhouse. The gift grew in the preparation and conveyance of it. Such a sweeping gesture was visible all round.

In the days when he drove wagons, Hora did this trip seven times. During the four-hour drive he would keep glancing back at his load, and having finally stopped outside the entrance to the institution, he would unload the Baron's beneficence with no sense of how slight it was.

Seven times he had found the poorhouse appealing. The inmates' jackets were of a material far better than canvas or drill. Well fed and with nothing to do for hours on end, they could chat in the dry corridors, sheltered from snow and cold. Their rooms were high and filled with bunks. There was a cross on the wall betokening peace and a bell served not to sound the alarm, but to summon them to their meals.

"Go and eat, the soup is on the table! – Your beds have been made, you can go and lie down!"

Having come to know this building, Hora could have wished for no more, and with no greater fervour, than to take up residence in it. To don a striped coat and eat garlic soup from a bowl that would be full to the end of time.

During the long journey, at moments of peace and quiet, this vision and this desire would keep coming into František's head. In the evening, as he chatted to Ber, Hora's longing would stir again and the old workman fell sad.

"I've forgotten everything," he said as he lay down on the same plank-bed he had once shared with Anna, "and I've got over it all." Out of a far corner his child said something back.

As he was dropping off to sleep, he heard the bell that hung beneath the cross and called people to the table. Opposite the window loomed the long-eared shadow of a horse, the stable fell silent and the grange slumbered.

Some fish-pond poachers were lying by the water, listening out for the whistle that signalled the end of the bailiff's round and the moment for them to cast their net. Some young thieves, so jittery that their hearts stopped beating, were squatting at the edge of a vast field of mixed corn and grabbing some by the handful. If the word *sin* is black, it was turning white, for nothing that can be put into words is so totally committed to wickedness for it to be pronounced over them darkly.

It is night, the eleventh hour is descending. An amorous gasp is the only sound and the only light showing is coming down from the windows of the Jew's tavern.

Very few people would have summoned up the fortitude with which to abide for years on end in rough dwellings and stables and to slave away on a manorial estate. But it is the lot of the poor to have their senses dulled and to wait an eternity. This penury is where they belong. They had their alehouse and paid it to be the bonfire on which to burn the last parings of their powers and the last remnants of their reason.

The inn at Ouhrov stood at the end of the village, concealed to the east by a line of gnarled plum trees, which was followed by a crooked fence that got knocked down with every brawl. One day, Lei, a Jew and proprietor of The Laid Table, had built it, muttering smug admonishments from his thick-lipped gob with a smile that was anything but sardonic. In not a single respect was The Laid Table worthy of its name. On the side next to the door the taproom had a handrail running along it, which was invariably damp and sticky, and it was one step higher than the rest of the place, so the Jew had a good view of anyone coming in for a drink. On the pewter top he would set out the calibrated glasses, adulterating the measures in the manner of one who knows that wealth is built on the small change garnered from occasionally selling short as the right moment presents itself.

The bare face of this innkeeper resembled a fist with the thumb overlapping it and slanting down to the third finger. He was bald, muttered things in a nasal twang whenever unsure of himself, he had no hint of a forehead and a hollow claw served him for a nose. He licked his chops with his two-faced tongue and he was stout enough to have sunk every gobbet of the fat that oozed constantly from his jowls. He happily called poachers by their first names, as he did those who owed his inn money, branding them with every foul epithet possible according to their sex and the magnitude of their destitution.

A pole nailed above the door into the hallway bore a disproportionately small signboard with a gaudily painted image of a green-clothed table and a tankard with a fish. A patron, having entered, could take his place on the bench. It ran round the walls like a low trough, longer by nine tenths than the two little tables along the sides. In this tavern people would drink themselves into a stupor, and its cellar was deeper than the graves of Smrdov cemetery. Men would enter through the door, which was narrow, for such are the gates of any heaven. They came in, stood at the bar and counted out their coppers to the requisite sum. Lei, leafing through a book or re-counting the crowns in his pocket, was in no rush to seal the deal; he could wait longer than the drinker's thirst.

On pay-day, there were several card-players in the pub, engrossed in their game, two butchers from the township of Syrová and no fewer than ten workmen from the grange. The Ouhrov ox handler, Řeka, a man of little wit, came in last.

The tavern was heading gently towards drunkenness and the halfwit, having sat down near the door, saw the light, the smoke, the stench and the voices of those assembled as heaven unbarred. He immersed himself in the Jew's tavern with the sense of a miser fondling his sack of gold, and his face was plied with an insane smile. Senses and passions shared this body between them and turned into beasts, each one charging in a different direction. He kept getting up and sitting down and, wave after wave, flurries of sheer delight set him all shaking, betokening his joy and hilarity.

"Where did you get the money?" Lei asked as he took the ox man's four florins.

"For one day's work!" he replied, putting every ounce of his willpower into the words. He wanted to reach out a fumbling hand and hold on to the Jew and tell him:

"Stay, maiden, dragon and thou, fish, seesawing in the smoke and the light above thy bottle! Stop, that I may tell if thou art the selfsame as I have seen in the shops of Hradec and above the grocer's counter at Jílová! Stop swaying this way and that and be still! Today I have money enough to pay for holding thee up and pawing thee."

"I'll make this crappy place of yours mine!" This much he managed to spout out loud again.

"Have a drink!" said the publican, handing him a glass that he downed in one gulp.

The Jew had said all he was saying and the money was in Gehenna.

If he lets him have another drink, he swore by the Great God, this idiot will never pay up and four florins are too little to cover his debt. However, when Řeka does start begging, gibbering the words of the Lord's Prayer, the one he knows best, and the countenance of the tavern turns towards the pair of them, when the players look up from their cards and all talk hushes, Lei relents and gives the ox man another glass and finally, given that the moment is opportune, grants him credit.

"That bloke," the giant Holub said, pointing at Řeka, "gets pissed just seeing the publican peeing. And yet all roads lead him to the pub." One of his cronies nodded in agreement and said: "It's that accident he had back when he was at school!"

The men were sitting in groups, only speaking now and again. The card games weren't going well and there were few reasons to start a fight. As they lapsed into silence, the publican, to keep night well clear of The Laid Table, pitched in a bit of noise with his gramophone.

If the tavern had been a sailing ship and Lei its captain, he would surely not call the hope springing within this silence a favourable wind. The place only stirs with heartache and only the Boreas of poverty carries it through a Saturday night. The hubbub was just enough for each of the workmen of Ouhrov to be in no doubt as to the paltriness that would endure forever and ever.

To speak of hope is pointless. A new spring exactly replicates springs past, the same sowing, the same herding, six barren days and a single Saturday. The summer followed by the same hungry, wretched winter. No one possesses a thing apart from this hostelry moment that re-counts a handful of coppers. Grab it by the horns and drink, my friends!

Inside Řeka's head the certainty of the moment sprouted gradually through the grey of first light. He gave someone's hand a vigorous shake and, uttering one of his inanities, took a sip from the butcher's glass. The only reason they forgave him his presumption was that they could more readily poke fun at the ass. Someone slapped the ox man on the back and bawled:

"Let's drink, let's drink together!" And the tempestuous spirit that would forever rise then pass away within this hellhole floated off over the heads of the drinkers like a she-eagle hovering over an army. Someone was roaring away like a singing hammer, and with every moment that passed the abandon just grew.

They went back to their cards, and Lei came trotting back with the money-pot and they played.

"Here's some money," said the butcher, slamming his fat purse down on the table. "You can bet up to a hundred and take the place apart!"

The flat and uninspired play drew a few glances towards the table, but the centre of the carousing and of that night remained the halfwit, who was staggering along by the benches and shouting. He resembled a giant clown, determined to destroy himself at all cost before the audience dispersed. He whined at the blows raining down on him and belched into people's glasses. His shirt was hanging out and his agonised heart, repeatedly laid bare, threshed about, sounding like a galloping hoof. One joker smeared him with a gobbet of spit and strings of saliva dangled from his forehead like the tassels of a crown of shame. Crazed, and despite all the ignominy, he maintained a kind of dignity of sickness and death.

As cocks began to crow, the inn began to empty, and Lei, not for the first time, bundled the ox handler out of the door.

Next day, the women in the stable, who'd been to the grog-shop to join their menfolk, gave an account of what Řeka had done. How he had screeched, how he'd been jerking off, with his penis out and his pants sopping wet. They were happy with the night, because their men had only got half-drunk, if noisily, but mindful of the women present; the outlay hadn't gone over what was normal and it hadn't been necessary to fight over the last florin. Their husbands hadn't lost their tempers and hadn't shown them the door, there was no coming to blows and Lei had treated them like ladies.

So the night, over which they might have wept, hungry, for a week, if it had been not Řeka, but one of their own men who'd gone over the edge, had been a good one.

"I couldn't stop laughing," said one crone with a gleam across her ugly features, "seeing the sod jigging about under Lei's lamplight. He was hopping about, kicking his legs as high as his shoulders, and then, just as he was standing on one leg, my old man came up, grabbed the dancing leg by the hock joint and made it hop the whole length of the taproom."

Meanwhile, Řeka the ox handler, whose inebriation had begun to slacken, was getting to his feet the other side of the tavern fence. The darkness in which he was swathed initially accompanied him. He might have put it that some god of hard liquors had tipped his heaven down towards the earth so that the drunken Řeka might alight. The shine on the drinker's face and his contentment would be his expression of thanks. He strode off, treading the dust of the road, and a flash of sunlight fell on him, making him blink and raise an eyebrow.

When he entered the gate, the steward Chot spotted him and, recalling all the fun and games at the carousal that he'd heard about, he turned across the yard towards Řeka, stepped up close to him and said:

"You're the most famous of all idiots. They tell me you were drinking from other people's glasses and that you stank worse than at any other time. The two butchers gave you a glass and you carried on as if you were drinking at your own expense. Where's the sheaf binder, and how much do you owe this time?"

"Aah," the ox man replied as he recalled the butcher's pouch, which had sprung open as it landed on the table, "I saw so much money. If I had that much, I could stay in the pub and drink without stopping."

At that point, the poor fellow, snake-bitten by the craving for money creeping up out of the depths of his poverty and puerility, froze, and he remained motionless as if already coated in gold coins that burned like fire and prickled like frost. He imagined that he could raise a hand and pick any one coin from his armour plating and Lei's tavern would be his.

Before he came out of his stupor, the steward was already making to leave. "Just shove off now!" he said, turning his back on him.

Řeka picked up his pitchfork and trudged off across the yard, his mouth filled with saliva and his craving reanimated.

At birth, people of Řeka's kind, halfwits, are made flesh. They are earth angels, unlike the cherubic, high-minded beings who are made of mere soul. Řeka could only do one thing at a time, so whenever he needed to think, he had to stop mucking out.

"The butcher's pouch full of ducats! I could sit about in our Ouhrov pub and day would never dawn and nights would never end. I could drink from every one of Lei's glasses. I'm going to have that belt, he's been a butcher for quite long enough. I'm going to be just like him so I can hang about in the pub and drink.

"I'll go now and undo the belt he has round his loins. But if he shouts out, I'll strangle him with a rope. If he makes a fuss, I'll stab him, and if he's asleep I'll use an axe."

The fallow ox snagged his chain with one horn, making it jangle, and, raising his head above the other one's neck, gave voice, long and drawn-out. Řeka came out of his musings and, as he left the shed, he paused at the threshold to whet his knife. The woman who peeled potatoes and cooked for the stables came along with a stool, a ball of wool and a needle and started mending her coat, because winter was nigh. Řeka stayed and rambled on about the vastness of time, about diseases, the harvest and good food. His knife was now sharp and he was making up his mind to kill Lei the next day.

"Can you tell me," he asked the woman, "where I can find an axe that's heavy and really sharp? I've only got a knife and its blade's too narrow."

CHAPTER TWO

The manor house at Ouhrov, a terror-stricken edifice abounding in the twists and wilfulness of the Baroque, reared up on the western slope of a hillock that went by the name of Noonday Witch. The constant repetition of the crinkled, inept proportions of twice thirty windows, blank and bleak, untouched by the sun at any time of the day, left the façade rather bland. The steps up to the main door faced east, which, with respect to the lie of the river, put them on a higher plane. Staring out in the same direction was the baronial coat of arms, like a blind eye staring out of a wrinkled face.

With the briskness of early morning, set in train by the hustle and bustle of horses, the servants' quarters below stairs would come to life in inanities. Where faineance reigns, men tend to be absent, and Ouhrov was devoid of them. From its foundations to its crimsoning roofs, this house was in its death throes and growing sordid; silence reigned in its slumbering chambers, no sound penetrated from without, and behind the second door you could still hear the rustle of the pages of the book being read by the old baron. By seven, the domestic staff had long finished their chores and hence could chew some hardtack till midday or sleep away till lunchtime. In the footwear of eavesdroppers they could pass through one room after another to arrive standing behind the baron. They knew what worried Danowitz, and also what a dirty old man he was. The noblesse and the mores of the barony, the manor house and the three hundred years that the Danowitz line had held Ouhrov belonged also to them.

Baron Maxmilián, who, outside the house, had nothing to commend him over any other sexagenarians, acquitted himself quite deftly at table. He had the gift of good manners and with ease, with delicate moderation, he could scoff a feast all by himself, just like Field Marshal Radetzky, who, having bought himself a litre of beer, used to do likewise. The baron resembled a wisp of straw that had risen on long legs and could walk. His face began with the clump of his protruding jaw; then, heading down the middle, making abrupt movements back and forth and up and down, was the peer's breath-filled nose. Danowitz's barony was the real thing, for he had always had food a-plenty and his coffers were quite easily kept full. Ouhrov, Sloup and Stráně were not all that he owned: he had forests in Galicia and a stud farm at least as big as Ouhrov, and yet he never spent money with a careless, imperishable gentility. He would wrangle in earnest over his revenues; compared to his, the meanness of the Jewish publican, Lei, was as a toadstool withering at the foot of a tree.

The timorous and grimy glint of the scaling-ladder was on the wane. What Ouhrov should have had on its arms was the dastard's slippers and a thief's skeleton key to betoken the events that unfolded in the summer of 1914.

Having returned home from Pest, Maxmilián fell ill following some horrendous drinking bout of aristocratic proportions, and, bewailing the cost of having loosened his purse-strings, he was preparing to take a rest. Three thousand had lodged in the stocking of some actress, whose antic was to scream from the edge of the stage then faint and weep and then go back to laughing; three thousand were left behind at the hotel, which, like a sewer, soaked up drink and vomit. They had drunk themselves into a near-stupor all the way to the old women squatting outside the lavatories. For three days, colourful liquor had gurgled down throats and for three days the tongues of the tosspots had roared.

The baron brought his head home between his knees, but he did arrive safely. The standard was run up its tall pole and the servants, carrying out his last will and testament, readied his bath and his bed.

He had entered the house bringing with him the heroic pain that was setting his head on fire. In the silence, the dying embers of his mind just might have flared up again. He was about to crash his head into the pillows, piled high, and sleep until all the bad smells and all the dust of intemperance had been exhaled.

The tip of the scaling-ladder has been turned against Maxmilián, since his two sons are rowing, and demanding money.

"I'm getting old," he said when they entered. "I'm a sick man and yet I still have to sort out the stupid, boorish things you keep doing. Have you no better ways of amusing yourselves?"

"I could think of plenty," said the elder son, "but I lack the means to take them up. And anyway, I can't conceive of calling this discussion amusing."

"What *is* the matter?" the old baron asked, pursuing a thought that was galloping ahead. "Go on, then, get on with your grievances, because I don't have time to waste, unlike you, sitting around here while your regiment's on the move, and you, too, who haven't been anywhere near your church in three months."

"No call for that," said Josef, "I know what house is most in need of a priest."

"I'm sure you do," he replied. "Your indolence is more like a virtue than the Church prescribes. You're a lie-abed and a pale reflection of heavenly sleep; this light of a heaven that remains open like a fence's swag sack makes you blessèd in Ouhrov. But dear, oh dear, within your order, despite such indomitable saintliness, all you are is a fool."

"Pah!" went the second son, "I can see no point in listening to all this; there is none, because we've heard it all before."

Enraged, the baron went across to the window, and, having glanced at the mould that had spread along the balcony woodwork, came back.

"Yes," he said, "let's get to the point. What do *you* want, Ervín?"

The officer meant to respond at length, for he believed in the nobility of his descent, and that belief afforded him a measure of composure. All it needed was to hold back time for the little runt to become a paragon of all that is baronial, and Ervín, settled in an armchair and, desirous of dignity, spoke like a glutton enjoying an enormous lunch. But Maxmilián was sick of the game. "I can let you have some money," he said, "but what you're asking for is too much."

The soldier repeated his figure: "Ten thousand," and the baron, raising three fingers of his left hand like a trident, insisted: "Three thousand!"

"At my age," Ervín went on, "certain things probably do come cheaper. I pay Kereta a tenth of what you'd have to pay for her, but this sop overrates me."

Before he could open his mouth again, Josef the priest rose and, jabbing a finger in the direction of his brother, yelped as if he had just burned his fingers.

"You shut up," the soldier responded. "Have you come to start blustering and squawking again? Are you looking for the right fiery word or are you being gnawed at by the bugs you've accumulated in your curate's den?"

"To hell...," said the old baron, turning his apoplectic face, with its seven veins strung into a knout of wrath, towards his younger son: "to hell with all the damn' claptrap you keep trotting out of your gabardine sleeves!"

Laughing, Ervín stepped up to his father, then, removing his monocle, glanced at himself in the mirror.

"I worry that one day Josef's going to clamber up onto the horses' trough and preach a sermon in the stable," he said as he and his father left the room together.

The zealous cleric was now alone. He folded his unclean hands in his lap and fumed.

Having finished grammar school, Josef Danowitz had entered the Order of the Knights of Malta, though anything but of his own volition and without duress, Baron Maxmilián had suffered some losses at cards and. having given a moment's thought to Ouhrov, whose waterlogged fields had long needed draining, he decided to make Josef a seminarist. Ouhrov, Sloup, Stráně and the property in Galicia were not big enough for three barons, two of whom, as they grew into maturity, would certainly increase the demands on their father's estate and go on to demand cash in the thousands.

One time, when the violins had stopped and a thunderous diapason had shot up from the brass, Maxmilián raised his gambler's hand with a sense of relief redoubled.

"My son Josef," he said to the drunkard beside him as the latter leaned over his glass looking for the centre point of his belly in it, "that same Josef I've told you about before, is entering the Order of Saint John of Jerusalem."

"So much the better," the drunkard replied, beholding Rhodes and Malta through his whimsical eyeglass.

The moment he reached that conclusion, the inertia began to pass. Some tart headed away from the bar, flaunting a smile on her mug the way a clown wields a stick. Her shadow darkened the jolly glass and the sage had to look up and away from its marvels. He and the girl entered into a ludicrous dialogue, largely effaced by the din of the music.

The arrangement conceived in a Vienna pub was not to be subverted by anyone now.

Until the moment when the baron communicated his wishes to his son, Josef had not been particularly devout. He had grown up at the margins of his tutor's care, which went not a handspan further than his measly remuneration warranted. He had been a weedy infant and his childhood passed in constant apprehension. The aspect of things, polyglot Vienna, then Ouhrov again, which had nothing to it but the tide of time, the plumes of pigeons, the frantic lament of cattle lowing and the firmament, streaked from time to time with silence and flashes of lightning – all this had left him stupid.

Providence, if seized by some matter or other, invariably lights a comical sign on the faces of teachers to become a lighthouse amid the inanities that are the waters in which they move.

Dörnek, Josef's educator, was famed for his nine-bristled wart. Nine, the number that pauses breathless before the solid presence of ten, was certainly not the final cause of Josef's insecurities. His gaze was forever drawn back to the lustrous bristly array whenever he had to recite irregular verbs, poems and even geometric formulae. He grew quite tense whenever he saw the all too worldly glutton run the back of his hand over the orb, surely only on loan to him from God, and was afraid of laughing when this comical eye turned out to be two lashes short.

Josef learned three languages and had struggled to ingest a little Latin. The toothless jaws of such bletherers as Cornelius Nepos clattered away on his desk, Father Cicero shrieked, flourishing periods like a fox its brush, the dogmatic Caesar used the *accusativus cum infinitivo* to state that "a thing can exist", but poets were silent. Having scraped through matric, Danowitz, dazzled within by the glory that had come to him so easily, began contemplating a work of solid scholarship.

"I'd have a room with four walls, composed entirely of books, and in the evening, having settled down by my lamp, leaving the crescent moon to carve a path through the night sky, I could turn some mystery or other into a patent truth."

Such creaky daydreaming is but a precarious pinion and Josef would gawp with his bloodshot eyes into the candle flames without seeing as far as the tip of the tiny tapering light and without taking wing. His sleep loitered in such thoughts as the night scurried by, devouring one hour after the next.

Blithe fools bend their angular heads down to their navels, which split open and devour them. Josef might have been eaten by the chink in his own belly, but his luck was grievously lacking.

One time, between taking a ride and his midmorning snack, the old baron, dusting off a speck caught between the folds of fabric on his knee (for he had just come back from the Frenchwoman's room), remembered the church and said: "Some of our relations and I have been talking about the future that awaits you, and, not without much deliberation and some uncertainty, we've decided to send you to a monastery."

"Me?" said the young man, flattered at the prospect of a long and impassioned discussion of his affairs. However, Maxmilián, in the right and proper manner of libertines not given to excessive parental care, nodded briefly and made to leave.

His horse was ready and Maxmilián, once astraddle, easily forgot what he had said.

After a two-hour discussion, Josef would certainly have come round and, making a virtue of his helplessness, would have hauled himself off to the remotest monastery with all the grace of obedient sons, whereas now, with the room deserted, he felt regret over the loss of the world he had not known. Hopelessness generally seeks an audience, and the emotions pouring forth from the iniquity stiffened his resolve.

That evening, at what seemed like an opportune moment, he spoke up in tones that already resembled the voice of a priest.

"Father," he began, standing amid the smoke of Maxmilián's cigarette, "I have in mind something different from what you have determined. I'm disinclined to abandon my secular studies and all the things that I've barely begun. You have misinterpreted my inclinations. I *could* become a priest, but only with regret and at the expense of a talent that points in the opposite direction. So, I don't wish to be one; I shall stay with my books which, though not prayer books, are in no way ungodly."

"Oh really?" Maxmilián responded, blowing smoke as far as the tips of the flowers stuck in a vessel in the middle of the table. "Really? You don't seem to have shown much sign of any particular aptitude. You've always been just hunched over a book, biting your nails and stirring compassion."

"You can," said Josef, "be quite indulgent sometimes, but when you're talking to me, you're always so angry and reproachful without cause. Is not this observation entirely apt when I've just completed a task that would be far beyond Ervín's faculties?"

"Yes," Maxmilián's French concubine concurred, setting her inestimable coiffure dancing, including the glacial moon that shone from it as it bode its time till nightfall. "Thinking over some of your actions, I'm of one mind with Baron Josef. Yes, my lord, without knowing it, you are a biased judge."

She spoke for Josef and against Ervín, since Josef was a poor ugly wretch of whom not even the old man could be jealous.

"Hell and damnation!" Danowitz bellowed, trying to stifle the rising imprecations: "You're talking rubbish and here am I, listening to you as if you just might articulate more than a sound like a door banging or the footsteps of the milkman clattering along with his churn. Do shut up! Enough claptrap! I didn't ask your opinion, and, Madame, I wasn't seeking a reference from you!"

So saying, the Baron bore his wrath out of the dining room and soon slept it off, though Josef was confoundedly dispirited by his father's high-handedness.

That autumn he joined the order of knighthood, having never dared repeat even so much as he had already said. Bent over a book full of romance, he hearkened to the distractions of his suffering in lifeless melancholy, uttering nothing but long, long sighs.

At about that time, three or four volatile moods were swelling up inside the Ouhrov manor house, sentiment and nostalgia being the major ones. The old baron gave Josef a kiss as a token of reconciliation, the Frenchwoman managed some seemly tears, and the women on the estate, in whose ownership is the mystery of conception and mortal love of the Virgin Mary, bewailed the sacrifice made, as if it were an actual sacrifice, bloody, too.

One day in late summer, Josef rode out with his father in a carriage drawn by sorrel stallions, and Ouhrov opened to let the equipage through, never to return. Maxmilián meant to give the two horses as a present to the prior, though he had puzzled long over how the gift was to be contrived. In the end, he decided to leave the novice's carriage to the priory as well, for he found great meaning in nothing's having its return.

Several boys ran after the carriage; the beggars lining the road were praying the Angelus in their scrawny voices, for noon was just being rung, and women stood in their doorways. The Smrdov parish priest, who had been fetched to embrace Josef thrice and thrice to kiss him, now turned to the Frenchwoman and said in his own telling voice: "The Baron could have dispensed with these sentimental niceties; they're ridiculous." Then he made his farewells and set off back, wiping his sweat away with the flat of his hand, because he was thrifty and was having to make his way home on foot.

Josef remained four years at the priory, renowned for nothing but its antiquity. He was as virtuous as those who had found faith in Jesus Christ, and like the rest he did a little evil even at prayer. He would fornicate in his mind and, arising from his sin, he would weep well into the night, which was minded to metamorphose yet again into the bed of a whore.

In this mansion of hypocrisy, which, all things considered, could hardly accord his torment any recognition, Danowitz was a bad advocate of his cause. Long-nosed, black priests and red, priests thin as snakes and priests with paunches all looked with a certain aversion at this man of feeble mind, this 'basher' as they called him for the way he babbled one prayer after another in his unremitting dread.

"Is it arrogance that makes him want to be a travesty? Does he want to give his stupidity the badge of sanctity?"

Josef would respond with a sense of the hollowness of his responses. Any items he touched with his flesh were no less mysterious than the blustery words, the hopes, anxieties and other states of his insensate spirit.

In his fifth year Josef became curate at one of the order's rectories and there he failed yet again.

"Good God, man," the old priest said to him, thinking of his embarrassing penances, "what is it, for God's sake, that makes you so flaunt a wickedness with which you're not even afflicted? The penitence and praying that you inflict on yourself presuppose sins a thousand times greater than such as might be committed by a whole marauding army. Does Providence not forgive any lapse against the Commandments after just the time it takes to say the Lord's Prayer and show some contrition? Take me, for instance, an old priest and a simple soul, I eat and I drink, but without mortifying my flesh to the detriment of the office which I am bound unto God to perform well, and yet I have hope of eternal life."

The virtues that had taken hold of Josef during his time in the priory dragged him through all their fallow lands. He was well deserving of the rage and resentment to which he was treated.

Having spent time in two parishes and held a curacy for which he had no understanding, Josef Danowitz had bolstered his sanctity, or the reputation for madness that followed him as the tinkle of a cowbell goes with the steps of its cow. Priests were sick of his company, for he knew neither how to speak, nor how to keep quiet. This petty curate took literally the nonsense and the medievalism that priests served up to them at seminaries with a kind of ironic circumspection. He delved into the lives of saints as if they were real lives and deeds and as if they could be multiplied by actions of his own. He followed prose narrative and poem, failing to notice the admonitions on which a good priest who knows his job can speak for two hours without touching on such terrible, alarming fictional portrayals as the body speared or the blood that runs free in lives of this kind. Josef Danowitz, a simpleton born too late to become a saint, was no less an inconvenience in the priory and parish rectories than he had been at his Ouhrov family seat.

Baron Maxmilián, having sorted things out with Ervín, went back to his younger son, but when he entered, Josef did not look up. Maxmilián glanced at the back of the curate's neck and his bloodless ears, which resembled two shards stuck into a pumpkin, and gave vent to his displeasure: "I've paid no heed to your blathering and I expect you're too busy to repeat any of it. Which is all the better since good things come in small doses, as the saying goes. However, I did gather that not even you can get by without your father's money."

Josef's ugly face quivered like a target that's taken a hit at a shooting gallery. "I wanted to ask for the money that is my due."

"Pah!" said Maxmilián, regaining his composure. "You're the second son, that's to say the youngest son and a priest to boot; are these reasons enough for you to be so presumptuous?"

Josef did not respond, his staunch sanctity having crooked his neck, and he remained silent.

"I meant to leave on horseback," he said, having eventually found his second wind, "but if nothing at Ouhrov is mine, I shall leave on foot."

"Of course," said the old baron, "you can trail from house to house, from parish to parish, in the manner of mendicant friars, and I'm sure that that way will lead you to the bishopric that you deserve. Your wayfaring will be splendid and I bet a hundred to one that you will go either to Rome or to the Holy Land."

"I'm going *from* this house."

"I've seen you off ten times before, and you've always come back before I recovered from my sorrow." So saying, old Danowitz crossed his arms and Josef rose. He was like one who has paused before coming to a decision, but he said not a word.

All Josef had wanted when he went to his father was a sum sufficient to enable him to live in Vienna and spend five or six months on the vain, nay ridiculous, endeavour with which he had been seized. Josef was one of those men who have neither the verve nor the powers to work on contemporary matters. Truths long past their time and as sham as a sword that no one has drawn from its rusting scabbard, truths whose time has passed and whose battle is over, skeletons of a sort, with their limbs broken on the wheels of martyrdom, a cadaverous past, all that is old in a world of workers who create, like God, towns or, like the silkworm, silk, workers who create machines and crops from the land, all that is old – a sort of graveyard of the Middle Ages – had cast a stray droplet from its tempests into the face of this, its posthumous child. The life of St Ursula of Dumnoia had been enough to drive Josef crazy. He was in ecstasy at the story of the saint from Assisi, with no understanding of the miracles that are brought forth even to this day.

At the very word Jerusalem Josef saw himself traversing a world that is space itself.

He is on his way, with naught but Satan standing at his right hand and God at his left. With every step, he kicks up dust and bounces the bundle on the end of his pilgrim's staff. All he has is his book. He is off and away. This moment is the impulse that he has found.

The rays of this vision now stretch as far as the palm trees, the flat roofs and the very hills of Zion. The road echoes to his determination and his steps resound to his every deed. He will be leaving, he will be off on his way. This unhorsed rider will stride on past milestones, through villages and towns, leaving wonderment behind him. He will make haste.

Mind now! Here beginneth the irreversible pilgrimage, the pace, the walking, the peregrination. And the trail is uneven, hilly, forested, clayey, arduous, unblazed, muddy, infernal and urgent.

CHAPTER THREE

The lugubrious door of St Theresa's Cathedral, that wart of religious zeal on the city's countenance, is just opening. The crossbar has fallen with a crash and, swinging out above the flight of steps, the shadow of the door leaf has touched the ground, one corner picking out a woman who is hurrying past. Vác Street, once The Fosse, the street of the yokels who brought their well-stuffed bundles here three hundred years ago, is teeming with whores, each one as wretched as the next. The chain of lights bends at the end of the street, which is descending into dusk.

Now night has fallen, drunks have taken their places in the pubs, and the whores are having to make haste for each of them to secure a bedfellow for the night.

The one who was caught by the fleeting shadow is neither the most woeful, nor the most common. Having passed the church, this prostitute blenched slightly, her thoughts falling a bit behind her gait.

"St Theresa's, the church with my name," the silly thing said, looking back.

The disc of the clock set in the façade of the church was blank at this distance, but having seen it, Teréz began to make haste. Imprudence is generally a proper prerogative of one of her kind who has been caught, but as long as she is still free to graze where she will, as long as she may still walk alone, as long as she is her own woman, she is generally cautious. Teréz passed a policeman like a lady in a hurry, the Chat Noir now being close.

The doorman, with whom she would sleep at not infrequent times of necessity, said Hello, but she left his familiarity unremarked and went in, head held high as if she were brash and beautiful.

The glare of the five chandeliers that marked out the demesnes of the five waiters blinded her and her entry was somewhat shaky, not quite befitting a whore of her distinction. No one came hurrying up to her and she could not say one word of the kind usually said upon entry. Her hat with all those silly things poking out of it, a hat that was meant to signal mettle, cast a dark and sorry shadow across her face. She resembled an old hag who, in her declining years and in spite of her trade, still manages to get pregnant.

Buda, city of open gates and four towers, a city of which soldiers, as they return to the forests and the fields in the plains, will speak as if it lay in the bosom of the world. Here the night is threaded through by a thousand fires, it is awash in purple, brocade, violins and quick temper. There are some thousand nightclubs in Buda, some thousand lakes of fire. And yet, come morning, the street sweeper of this rubbish dump will count no more than seven Catholic sins. The Madonna abides in images of her, parliament is blethering away in a slightly mournful session at this time, and the Danube flows down, while the countless brothels are oh so conventionally ready on heat. In matters of boozy nights out, there are no shortfalls here and the Chat Noir is certainly well suited to any urge to drink.

A looking glass confuses the premises with a picture, and looking into this fiery furnace, you will put a foot wrong.

The overflowing honeycomb of the bar will rise to the height of mountains, streams of wine will be released from bottles as yellow and dark as China and Ethiopia. The hour of debaucheries, toxic substances and fornication is nigh. Strike, strike the pewter top and set the strings vibrating in fours! Fiery drum, flute and the most tumultuous blare!

The whore Teréz sat down next to a man, uninvited. He was drunk, and his perception was almost burnt out.

"The smallest of all," he said to another drinker, who was propped against his easy chair, "the smallest of all miracles is this wisp of straw. I knew her way back when she went under five different names."

Having wet her lips in the wine of this living witness to her past, who could still see things despite his obnubilation, Teréz began to speak and was very much the whore.

"My colours are white, gold and green. Hence three of my names, but I cannot utter either the fourth or last."

Who has taken a fancy to playing with a bow? The left arm of the bowman rises to take aim and the animal can be seen crumpling at the knee.

An excess of light was opening out through the chinks in which darkness flickered. The night, rising into a shimmering circle, cast sparks in the blaze, and all the yelling and the hubbub of people talking, sounding like sirens under maximum compression, rang out with a sudden sharp cry.

"Éljen!"

A deep shaft of passions opened wide and at the heart of the fury, twice or thrice, the face of Teréz became visible.

Her deathly pale beau had finally fallen asleep, but this handmaiden of love was still not leaving yet, for the sleeper was propped against her shoulder. It was nearly dawn. She eased the scruffy drooping cloth aside with her foot. Day was approaching and the looking glass was ceasing to see. This was the hour of dishwashers and milkmen. Cold was drifting down in the sheaves of light and a cigarette case glistened with frost.

"Up you get," the whore said, having touched the man's face. "Get up, I want you to take me out of here, get up, you can't sleep in the Chat Noir right through till tonight."

The sleeper came to and went through all his pockets. "If you haven't left yet, I must have got everything," he told his doxy. "Surely you're not waiting to bring on your shower of tears, are you?"

"Pah!" she replied, "I'm not squalling, I've seen quite enough broken skulls to have become this shadow of the woman I once was. You used to say I could come and see you any time I wanted. So let's be going. The time is now."

Meanwhile Teréz's lover had donned his blouson, tossed aside in the middle of the night, and now, looking into the whore's compact mirror, he set about washing his face with his pocket handkerchief.

"All right," he conceded, without turning his head, "let's go if you want to be what you once were. Perhaps I'll hear your old names again, for I still live in the same house."

Teréz put her coat on while the man paid the bill. They were treated to the effusive thanks of the waiters and the madam, who had all descended on the soldier's open pocket book.

"What a lovely day it is, sir; it's seven in the morning and a lovely day," said some domestic as he brought the soldier's cloak.

They took their seats in a hastily summoned hackney cab and left.

Now and again there was a squeak of blinds being opened like the gaping maws of animals, and bleary-eyed shop assistants were rolling their sleeves up for work. The coupé enclosed the remnant of the night and the streets of Pest barely touched its windows. The vacant and unmoving face of the city sped away behind them, bearing with it the last remembrance of the blandishments of the pub. At the corner of Kör Street, the driver stopped and opened the cab door. "We're there, sir."

The soldier being held up haggling with the cabman, the whore entered the house, but before she had even passed the concierge's lodge, he caught up with her and, letting go of his sabre, took her by the arm.

"Don't go inside, I was only joking."

"I've spent five years in my trade," Teréz replied as she stood there, "and no matter how paltry a trade it is, enough men have passed through for me to know what they're like. You might say I've worn a mask with a tangled mass of cotton wool, but who's ever caught me splitting without being paid after I've given a man a nightlong ride? I can explain it all to you, but let each see to his own pocket."

As she spoke, the soldier broke into a laugh, but since nothing ends so quickly in accord as laughter, he soon recognised the justice of what his whore had said. Being well known for his adventures and his brash demeanour, it was hellishly easy for him to make a scene of it.

"The time is ripe for action," he said. "Let's go and finish what we've been saying."

So saying, Danowitz set off up the stairs, taking them two at a time. If the fellow was unsparing to himself, why should he spare others? Everything struck him as happenstance, happenstance that could be shaped, twisted and disposed of so that he could eventually quit the game and stride blithely by.

Having opened the door to his flat, he crossed the hallway without even removing his cloak.

"Hello, Aranka, I've brought someone who's got something to tell you," he called mid-chortle, and when the door remained shut, he unbuckled his sabre from his hip and tossed it onto the floor.

This noisy act of immoderation failed to release the lock, so Danowitz had to look for the key. They finally entered the room. The light of an ordinary day was permeating the space and the whore was like unto herself. She was a poor woman.

"You're home, sir," she said, setting aside her hat, but Danowitz, whose wit was being fired by the delay, banged at the bedroom door until it flew open and replied: "Not until I'm in bed, ma'am, and then only if it's empty."

Woeful the names of whores and woeful the dignities conferred on them in the seasons of pimps. Two such women were standing there face to face, rehearsing the same shrieks, the same astonishment and the same sense of outrage.

"You're not alone, Ervín?"

"Far from it," he replied, repeating Teréz's name. "It's time for you two to meet on good terms. It's a time for reconciliation, given that no two tarts, neither of whom can sleep unless beside the same man, can go bitching about the other forever."

"I've nothing to say," said Teréz, "where's my hat?"

Ervín impaled it on the tip of his sword.

Aranka, the girl who had spent the last three weeks sleeping at Ervín's, tossed her cloak and, left almost naked, started putting on her shoes. The silence and the dingy window made the incident more embarrassing than it merited.

Teréz took hold of her hat and made to leave first. "I want my money," she said on the way out and accepted it without inhibition.

Aranka locked the wardrobes and, taking the keys with her, told Ervín: "I'll be back for my things at six. I believe you're usually not in then, so I won't run into you."

As they were leaving, the two women encountered the officer's servant and felt embarrassed at having been overheard. There was no difference between them and they each hurried away in the same direction. The strigine eye emblematic of whores – how it sparkles, a round window filled with lights, and yet unseeing. They may have seen the Ouhrov ploughman, who was standing in the baron's ante-room, but they ignored him. After a short moment, a brief stop, he would have said and done any one of a hundred things for their passage not to look silly. But they went on, leaving this cavalier as if his role of servant was just right.

Teréz went down the stairs, clutching her whore's skirts, and turned to hurl some abuse at the woman behind her.

"Pah!" the latter retorted, "stay with the ash-heap if you're minded to whine, go back for your dinners and the scraps I've left." They finally left the building and Kör Street split their hostility as they went their separate ways.

Meanwhile Danowitz had sat down to breakfast and his mind, ever apt to wander, gradually left the incident with the whores behind. The silence, permeated by the commotion of daytime, resembled a ruffled lake and started to engulf the day. Teréz was never to return to this abode, for being cast into oblivion engenders neither sympathetic, nor sentimental regret. Danowitz's bachelorhood is manly, and when the whore passed the corner of his house the following day, she did so in silence, uttering not a word, as if that bachelorhood harboured a command.

Having finished eating, Ervín rose and went out, leaving his mail untouched.

In the flow of the street, amid the inordinate beauty of children, he bore his ridiculous iron sword with not a hint of embarrassment. A column of heavy wagons had churned up the dust, which mingled with the smoke, and now, its bulk concealing the procession of porters and workhorses, it was heading in the same direction as the baron's footsteps. A rustic in leather breeches was standing right at the edge of the stream of traffic and Ervín, observing all these labours that fail daily in their purpose and in the matter of wages, was laughing. A girl brimming in rosiness and a lady in mourning passed by him and he weighed them up as if having to choose between them. After this deliberation and the drama of a world at work, Danowitz entered the sudden silence of a side street that led through its double bend towards the monstrous bulk of his barracks.

Having arrived at this architectural hybrid, all too frequently spurned in this part of Hungary, and with scarcely a glance at the barking sentry, Danowitz passed through the gate leading to the commandant's and the officers' quarters.

These spaces, of a gloomy whiteness and filled with laughter that, cast aloft, fell back down, these cubes as full of smoke as the barrel of a rifle that has just been fired, these spaces, always populous, always clamorous, had their own voice and their own manners.

Amid such an almost beautiful tumult it was impossible to think of two pages in a book opening to stammer out lessons of any kind. Brash boorishness and the blather that is called nothing and is nothing, became, among this pack, the order and idiom of the day. All the inconveniences of army life, all the inconveniences of affairs of the heart and all the inconveniences caused by money vanished in the dust of horseplay and the particular patois of the mess hall.

Attila at full tilt. The thunder of galloping hooves and tumultuous cheers making light work of the plain stretching all the way to the herds' distant waterholes. Volleys of verbal lightning. Tales of the tallest and bottles brimful of laughter! Such excitements were substantial enough to keep the gluttonous officers captive.

The door was like a rising sluice-gate and Ervín entered mid-flow.

"What whim kept you?" a young officer asked, turning to Danowitz, "I waited for you till long past midnight."

"Whim," Ervín replied, "I don't have whims that late, I just got drunk before I counted the hours, that's all."

A cavalry captain, already half-drunk at this sober hour, touched Danowitz's shoulder with his glove. "I don't mean to go by your clock, nor shall I invite you to go by mine, but if a drinker doesn't know what midnight is, he can't ever have been drunk."

"Who knows which of your glasses isn't filled with truth, and who knows which of your certainties isn't nonsense," said Ervín, drinking wine with the captain.

"I'm off, my friend, no nun has ever passed me by without me becoming a lecher at least for an instant, and no one has ever praised drunkenness in my presence without me damning it to hell."

The multifarious chatter was riven by a shout rising from the middle of the mess hall: "I'm sure I like her! I'm sure I like her!"

"Why not," they responded, "we don't intend to deny it."

The assertion was cried out with such force and the voice was so audible that it cut through all the clatter, the noise of stools falling and the tinkling of broken glass, and formed a star. Amid all the clangour no one remained silent, and the arena of noise raised its voice to a dizzying height. Someone left, leaving the door of the mill wide open. It was time to go about one's affairs.

Five or six officers settled down to a game of cards and the room gradually emptied.

Three o'clock was drawing nigh and the officers' lunchtime usually ended at two. Danowitz had to use a small table, brought in by an already agitated soldier, and eat in haste. He was alone, but the cavalry captain, irritated by some word that had been uttered, came looking for him. Finally spotting Danowitz, he entered the mess hall and voiced his exasperation at young men who, having barely got their feet under the regimental table, turn into louts.

Ervín, with foreknowledge of the discourse of drunken hussars, listened with indifference.

"I've got other things on my mind," he said with a dismissive gesture.

"That's as may be, but I mean you to see what I'm thinking," the captain replied. In the middle of his face, so befitting a hussar, his duo of moustaches bristled and twitches born of wrath half-bared a tooth which, despite the purposes it served, was not a fang.

A sudden silence amplified this whole incident and rendered it visible from all sides. The other ranks still left in the gaming room and the adjacent hall could see, through the open door, these cocks with their hackles now raised. One man stood up, dying for an invitation to join in, which was bound to be forthcoming, while another, sick of all such distractions, which were ludicrous to the point of making one weep, turned away to show just how bored he was.

"There are days," said Danowitz, without ceasing to eat, "when you are unbearable, but the moment you lack the wit to find one, you cast about for any pretext to start a fight, though I don't get angry with you because your red-headed asininity is undisputed."

"I'd need a stick to reply to that with," said the captain ceremoniously.

Danowitz rose to his feet.

"I'm not used to using sticks, but if it's not too much trouble for you to take up your sabre tomorrow at five, we can settle the matter."

So saying, Danowitz, mindful of his regiment's mores, bowed, then he went out to the squadron that was waiting for him.

"Pah!" said the hussar with an ironic bald patch down the edges of his sideburns, "all this is just sheer posturing. With reconciliation and compromise, the point of a sabre would be unlikely to snick a single artery! Reconciliation ending in carousal, which, once anticipated, could have settled this quarrel so clumsily contrived!"

Danowitz crossed the expanse of the courtyard to join his hussars. In their left hands his squadron held absent reins, while their right hands held their sabres aloft, configuring, in the *prime* position, a foolhardy, dazzling acting-out of the furies of war.

These iron pieces, enkindled in the gloom of the parade ground, will turn red with blood, for a kind of undeniable beauty has so confused this host of simple souls that they now quite like sporting the two colours of the hussars, sitting astride horses and flashing their swishing blades.

By Jove, Danowitz is their commanding officer and a good hussar!

Having received the guardsman's report and standing legs apart, he raises his heavy sabre and is about to act the giddy goat in front of his men, executing side-to-side swings as if he were a sower seeking to seed the dark clouds. They will all slacken and flag in the confines of the battlefield, but for now Danowitz is cleaving this Friday's imaginary body with the hundredth of his magnificent crosswise swipes.

His name will grow, for anyone can see that their sub-captain doesn't care two hoots about fear or the uncertainties of duels. There'll be plenty said in the sleeping quarters and the affair will achieve greatness for being partly kept under wraps and for Danowitz's dauntlessness.

CHAPTER FOUR

The reaper's temples, drenched in tears of sweat during bursts of the recurrently lost summer, would not dry off. Such teardrops are saltier than all the seas and of all rednesses the reddest.

There were nights and again there were days. There were noontides when these working men dashed to the stream to sink their lacerated forelimbs in it. Field labourers are too pain-stricken to speak, and, wounded by their own long silence, they resemble a grave in whose depths a bleeding heart still stirs. In silence they let their crops mature and the yelp with which they seek release from time to time is naught but lamentation.

The flagon that some, doubtless sober, arch-scallywag had hauled along to fire the men's morale, emptied itself into their throats and the low sun redoubled its searing. One lad, who inspired pity because his frame was still unresponsive to work, desired a drink. He waited unspeaking and making no gesture. Nothing came his way but the dubious dignity of standing two steps from the reapers' vessel, and yet he did finally find his voice in an oath far more resonant than an entreaty.

At harvest time, Hora forsook his outbuildings and went out with the others into the bountiful fields, somewhat confused by this season, which had him interrupt the flow of his favourite thoughts and see new things. In the cold quiet of a cowshed he could stare into the

depths of an image descried fifty years previously. Cob-webs quivering among the bars at the windows were a seal of secrecy.

He had gone forth from his fastness leaving the door wide open and headed alone out into the fields, the others disregarding him in order to avoid his spiritless yarns.

Flames cascaded out of the sun to the centre of a yellowish circle, gradually burning their intangible brand, and Hora, while his sense of foreboding ran ahead unaffected by anything seen, raised his blind gaze into this fiery furnace. His eternal agitation and, yet again, that sound born inside his head, the hideous shrieks of his body and its all too impaired workings, all these things escalated in the sun's ferocity. The old man saw the leaves moving in the treetops, without hearing their rustle or any other sound beyond what stirred inside him.

Having finally reached the steam thresher, the crip-ple might have taken a rest, but at that very moment the call to work came. The labourers sitting astride the restraining beams, axletrees and straps got up and the thresher, swathed in smoke to its very maw and sedate in the eternal twilight of its motion, unleashed its clatter as if about to take to the air. The cast-iron grew red hot and a column of jangling air rose above it. Countless people hauled freshly cut sheaves over to the toothed threshing cylinder. Swathers set out across the vast fields and the reaper set its crankshafts in motion, divider taking turns with cutter bar.

On this vast work-filled plain Hora was left groping, as if passing through a vault. His fleeting moments, interrupted by the past, moments of yelling, moments of the sound and the fury of machinery, were no longer a working day. This outsider would trip up on the very levelness of the field, while the others were fired up by their labours. Five men followed teams of horses and no fewer than twenty had gathered round the thresher. Of women there were precisely twelve.

"Don't go mad!" one man said to a young fellow who was rushing things.

"That's not," the latter replied, "the first time I've been given such advice, and yet who is crazier than one who stops to woolgather in the middle of the harvest or lounges about in every corner of the field?"

"Idiot," said the workman, looking fondly upon this greenhorn, who still had so little between his ears.

The day wore on, the stack grew, and each scythe had made nine trips. The womenfolk, bent over their armfuls of corn and elevating their backsides, were on the brink of exhaustion. They were going to have to lever themselves up hand on thigh in order to stand straight, and now someone's slapped them across their broad buttocks.

"Onwards and upwards, my lassies, must keep your pelvises in trim!"

This habitual practice gave rise to some less than pretty banter.

"Hora," one tall fellow shouted as he went off with his pitchfork handle resting on his shoulder, "Hora, I reckon you can't have forgotten about last night's dinner, eh? What were you saying as you drank from our jug? Today's no less hot than yesterday, so, shall we be drinking again?"

Hora would have preferred not to reply to this man who had shouted out his name so brazenly.

"I don't have any money except Saturdays," he said, "and even then I can't go buying beer. Wait till the overseer gets here with a flagon and drink my portion."

The overseer came hurrying past this harassment and the discomfited response to it and both voices were constrained into silence. The work was proceeding apace and the thresher, casting ever more sheaves onto the summit of the stack, was going full tilt while fixed to the spot.

Noon, anticipated from a far distance, was approaching only slowly. Hora was growing weary and kept injuring himself on bent spikes; he dragged his leg behind him, more unwieldy than a pig jerking at the butcher's rope on its way to the slaughter.

In another corner of the field, more elevated at this point, Řeka was at work among the other human wrecks. As his mind grew sharper, he weltered in the certainties of his labours almost like the others, for he was well-versed in his daily grind and he was adroit. And yet an idea – like a raven repeating his few croaks as he circles a workman's head – an idea, or some mere words, kept coming to the tip of Řeka's tongue.

"Riches! Riches beyond a heart's desire! I'm punished almost daily and every morning I pray. Our Father, who art in Heaven, grant unto me the money and treasures that thou keepest hidden. I shall match the good fortune of the pretentious, the good fortune of the brute who beats me even though I pay him the money he demands. I shall contrive such things as I have seen, having been inside the most affluent abode. I do not desire to achieve things by casting aspersions and I shall not speak ill of my lord and master, though I shall take what shall have been made ready and what awaits me. Spotting the axe that I have honed, he who seeks my downfall shall be humbled and abashed, he shall be turned back and cast into ignominy. Why does he drag his feet and not keep his word that I accepted? I have long been expecting him to think back, let him respond and face up to me!"

Breathing the murder upon which he was resolved, Řeka hadn't been able to hold back and had been speaking aloud.

"Who gave you his word and what are you expecting?" said Ber, laughing at the maniac's gory discourse.

"Riches shall be mine thanks to my axe," the cattleman replied, "and what I have sworn I shall put into effect. Come when it is done and you shall drink and you shall sit with me till morning and through to the next night."

"Tchah!" said Ber, shocked at the imbecility that had held him up, "you dimwit, I won't have you talking such drivel," and so saying, he hit him with the end of his whipstock.

Řeka fell silent, for he could but listen for the whooshing of wind and scythe and the stirring of acres of corn to echo what he'd been saying. He was not setting aside the enactment of murder; his mind was made up without his will having spoken.

Meanwhile the sun had climbed further and the day had reached its zenith. The whistle of the steam thresher sounded again. The oxen slowed their steps to a standstill and people, dropping whatever they were doing, went over to the water tub.

"I need a drink, damn it, I'm thirsty, fill the pot to the brim, never mind if it spills over, this isn't wine we're drinking." One of the women took some water in the palms of her hands, quite unperturbed that the others were going to drink from the container. It's too much bother and too long to wait, since we've only got one barrel.

Hora was among the last to step up to the tub, and having scooped out some water, he found himself drinking the dregs, since by then the tub was almost empty. "I didn't want to drink at midday anyway," he said, "it's far too hot and seven out of every nine ailments arise from this error of judgement."

Then, having drunk a jugful, he began to eat.

"Dear me," Ber said, "if you don't eat meat even at harvest time, you're being more than thrifty, and I'm sure you wouldn't think twice about drinking if the barrel contained not water, but beer, and I'm sure you'd scoff a whole ram if one were being doled out. You're always starving yourself and you're always thirsty, you save up your pennies and then start whingeing. I wish that twice-knotted kerchief of yours was mine; I wish I had the money bags of moaners."

Hora's face, that depository of disasters, reacted with dread and pride, which jostled for space in the gash that was his mouth. He held tight to his little pouch, strung round his loins and round his neck. The dimwit, who had sat down next to the old boy's feet, couldn't help thinking about his money again.

"Why wouldn't you eat anything that's good, and why wouldn't you drink? I shall have silver and gold pieces and I'll pour away a whole bottle of spirits into the cattle trough. Why wouldn't you drink?" he said, and when the men around started laughing, he repeated his inanity.

"Well," the reaper said, shaking Řeka, "well, wise-acre, couldn't you do something for us right now? Is today any worse than the day you're planning for? What do you need to work your magic? Are your snares fine and sturdy, or has the buck already been ginned?"

Meanwhile, noon was descending from its high peak and it was time to rise from the empty lunch-pails. The wheels of the thresher sprang back to life and fresh teams of horses took over.

The time for warbling had passed and in the middle of the field, gushing its black breath skywards, the thresher was clattering away. The reapers were on their last legs and they weren't going to march in parade as the last sheaf was borne into the overflowing barns. Their throats were well past shouting Hurrah! The mawkish horseplay was forgotten.

The thresher belted away till late and, having caught up with the night, called it a day. The workmen lay down their implements and headed for their homesteads.

Sixteen hours without speaking had passed and speech had almost been forgotten. Who had anything to say? The women, whose day was just beginning, for they brooked these labours as naught compared to the cooking of dinner, which still awaited them, and so the eternal culinarians hurried off ahead of the rest. None of them uttered a word and none sparked an argument. They left with their pitchfork handles on their shoulders, their feet sinking in the dust. One single thought impelled each one to hurry and scurry.

The menfolk dawdled and only the odd idle comment hopped across the rills of silence that divided them. Someone remarked that the days were getting shorter, and they all agreed, while the mad Řeka and František doggedly held out against any such trivia.

"Pah, who cares about piffle based on the calendar? As I see it, no one gets het up over withheld wages that land in your lap just as you're at your lowest ebb and can't even be bothered to cook. I couldn't care less about the changing seasons, provided Saturday's coming along again to cough up the readies I can't wait to get my hands on."

"Hell," said Řeka in response to his companion's wrath, "what a sly bunch they are! They're on good money and the pouches at their hips are bursting with grub. So it's winter from Monday to Saturday, what of it, doesn't time drag as it is and what's the calendar got to do with it?"

Meanwhile the men had reached the gate to the yard, which opened to admit them.

"I don't like to leave you in a fix," said Dudek, pulling the madman aside, "because your gob's awry and you'd never let up, so let me do something for you."

86

With that, Dudek sloshed a bucket over Řeka's head. He had plenty of time to laugh, because Řeka didn't fight back and kept angrily silent, uttering not so much as a word.

When darkness fell and the others were already asleep, Řeka ascended the box of an old carriage that, since some point, had been kept outside the shed, and on this driver's seat, elevated high above all ox handlers, he supped on bread. He cut doorstep rounds and chomped away at them between his hoggish jaws.

Meanwhile, in barn and rick, housemaids waited for their disconsolate paramours. At least for this moment their lovers took them with gross abandon. Hell, they could have shivered the shanks of these mares, who were no less frenetic and no less appetent in their puny passion. Yelping with gratification and going quite crazy, man and woman in the convulsions of coition, they did not relax their reeking embrace while there was still some blood in passion's stub.

Such fornicating was not alien to Řeka, but that summer there was no crone at the grange old and gross enough to take the lunatic to her bed of straw.

Having finished his bread, the stockman, feeling neither fear nor doubt now that his mind was made up, turned his thoughts to the job at hand. He was to commit a murder. All the thoughts that entered this body became the very substance of his state, or his right hand. And now his craving and his hand already raised demanded an attack. A blow struck.

Jumping down from the carriage, Řeka set about looking for the axe that was usually sunk in the chopping block by the log pile. Having walked round the pile of wood, he went back towards the draw shave that he'd passed previously, then having given a couple of spins to the grindstone he went off to find some alternative tool in the wheelwright's workshop or the carpenter's, which was open.

At last he found, under a saw-horse, an adze that the master carpenter had dropped there. It was old and would barely pass for the frenzied axe of assassins.

"Aha," said the stockman, inspecting the blade as he held it up against the moon, "aha, this isn't bad and perhaps better than the other things, being not so light." So saying, Řeka found a stick and, standing by the chopping block, chipped off one bit after another until only a tiny piece was left that he could barely grip between his fingers.

It was eleven o'clock. Řeka could have climbed over the fence and left the yard on the other side without bumping into anyone, but instead he crossed the open space to the closed gate.

The man sleeping there rose from his bench and seeing the fool, asked: "What are looking for? Why aren't you asleep, you loony?"

"What's wrong?" Řeka replied, briefly gripping the axe between his knees and raising his freed hands, "I've got a bad head."

The black beast was visible against the shining stars. He had no axe and could go, for the sleeper did not look up again.

He found the gate and side door locked, so he bashed the bolt with his blade, opened the gate and went out. He quickened his pace and only stopped when he reached Lei's tavern. It was in darkness. The Jew was asleep. Having arrived this far, Řeka went up to the door and tried the handle as if it were daytime and Lei were standing at his bar. The door wouldn't budge and Řeka was taken aback at this anomaly. Murder was not as easy as he'd been expecting.

"If he sleeps with the door locked, he must be richer than I thought," the stockman mused, "though I can't see why I should leave since no bolt is stronger than an axe."

For a few moments he hesitated, believing that Lei would rise from his bed and come out through the open door right under a death-dealing blow. But the Jew slept on and the solid lock didn't even budge. So the madman raised his arm and, pausing for an instant, aimed a blow at the door frame with his blade. But not even that din woke anyone. Lei may have sat up in bed and, propping his elbow on the bed frame, may have listened to see who it might be, maybe he would have risen, for the dogs were yapping a bit, but before he could reach for his candlestick, there were some more bangs, all too fierce and all too crazy.

Anyone banging like that can surely only be some drunkard demanding a last bottle and some final chit-chat, of which Lei had had his fill.

Řeka waited, and when nothing inside the building stirred, he made to return to the grange.

Midnight had come and gone and time had side-stepped the inept assassin, who'd been banging on the door having failed to spot an only part-closed window.

He was too stupid to calculate his act. The raised axe dropped vertically down to the assassin's knees and the innocent fool set off back. He found himself thinking about butchers again. However, having passed through the side gate, he forgot all about riches. He wanted to sleep and, crawling in among his rags, he clasped his arms round the axe that would be the key.

The pointed horn of the moon poking out from under a cloud, the horn of a heavenly bull, a wedge and a jab that parted the darkness, a jab full of luminosity or blood flowing down towards the madman, issued a kind of challenge one last time and the stockman, still intent on achieving his end, sank the axe, in a terrifying manner, into the ceiling beam above his head. He lay down with a slight thrill, clutching a fistful of straw.

Morning, sinking down out of a frosty world, too early for all the workmen, touched the foolish man with a single ray, and he made to get up. He didn't even recall the cleaver stuck up there in the beam, and, slightly dizzy and confused, went out to the water butt, by which Hora and Jakub were standing. He began telling them all about his nocturnal jaunt, but omitting the axe.

"Look here," they replied, "we didn't know you were so smart. Stick to good practice and grab a pitchfork, because Saturday pay, for all it's so meagre, is still better than the riches you're talking about. Do you think it's that easy to rob the Jew? Doesn't he keep watch, isn't his treasure chest made of iron and doesn't he keep his closet locked?"

"Pah, leave off," said Ber, "this ass won't do anything worth speaking of, he just can't stop running off at the mouth and that's all he ever does." And turning to the ox handler, he erupted into laughter, part scornful, part provocative.

Several workmen came out of the barrack and the womenfolk were rising to feed the animals.

It was five o'clock and work was commencing. Every last one of the labourers was now up, ready to work till suppertime. It is to the sounds of early morning that the strength to guide the plough and wield the scythe is born, no matter that the body, so wretched and sluggish, is still asleep.

Amid the fragile heads, Ber and Řeka were still talking round in circles, though Ber was at least able to take up a pitchfork to load fodder into a huge basket. Řeka hung about a few whiles longer and finally, behind as ever, he hurried after the others.

That day, not one whit different from the day before, had begun and was passing. Řeka was driven both to hurry and to dither over his determination to commit murder, and his customary shortcomings repeatedly annoyed the overseer, who was loitering in the area.

Meanwhile the axe was still stuck in the beam, waiting for nightfall, and no one who happened to pass the would-be assassin noticed his fearful unease and derangement. He picked up his pitchfork and waved it about. He jabbed with it and the sparks that rose in the darkness of the moment, five stars, five flames, stood still above the astounded head of the ox handler. The assassin hauled himself up to his full height, as if until that moment he had been some animal that does not walk erect. He stood, and a terrible glory and a terrible grandeur bore his hand aloft. He was the precursor of an armed force, he could take whatsoever he would, he could strike and beat those who did not deign to reply when questioned. He could consume all the money in the world, he could split the Jew's skull open with a single blow and ram his pitchfork all the way up to the handle into his twitching body. At last the poor man

could curse and swear, at last he was as mighty as a man in a rage. Yet not even now, at the brink of mercy and a lethal night, did anyone look up to see him. A mere imagining of his strength, a dumb show of death, might just have sufficed for the ox handler, if there'd been any onlookers. Perhaps all that was needed was for any one of those who had baited him to look his way and say:

"Look, our ox handler's up early, watch yourselves, because it strikes me he's not in a joking mood."

But the workmen did not look up at Řeka, not one, and the last moment when he might have brought down the axe already raised to strike had passed.

Around eight o'clock work was winding down, it was the end of the day and night was drawing a veil of darkness across the sky.

Řeka could go back to his axe. He was walking between beech trees and in his determination he bashed the trunks as he passed. The strength was returning to his arms. He was like a man whose words are reasonable and whose deeds are visible. A guise of calm and courage, a mask set upon the face of a madman who twists and turns in the turbulence of his spirit, an image of sapience, made the assassin's face terrible.

He entered the courtyard as darkness closed in. The corner of the stable where he slept was deserted and no one spotted Řeka as he stood on his bed, ripped the axe from the beam and, throwing all caution to the wind, crossed the yard and the manor house garden. A sound like that of a flame or like the afterglow of some word led him through the empty space, flaring and rustling again through the gate and down the path.

The main entrance to the house was not locked and Řeka entered, making no more sound than a barn owl.

The trashy sculptural group which dominated the hall from which the staircase rose, with its hollowed out features facing the door and a spiked blade in one raised hand, seemed to be acting as the guardian of the house. The assassin paused, raising his cap.

After a moment that did eventually subside, Řeka, giving the statuary, which frightened him, a wide berth and not letting it out of his sight, mounted the staircase to the upper floor. He opened the first door he came across and went through the room without so much as a pause. Finally he was in the antechamber to the baron's bedroom.

The profundities of the silence did not stir and the would-be assassin opened the last door. Having reached the baron's bedside, he stood briefly at the head, staring at some frieze, and seeing in it the image of a wounded man, a little donkey and those of whom the parable spoke, he could not stifle a yelp, for in it he had recognised the story of the Good Samaritan.

However, even this vociferation, quite loud enough to have been heard, attracted no one, since, at the very moment when the assassin entered his bedroom, old Danowitz, having come home from the hunt late that evening, had just gone into the bathroom. The baron had plunged his head into the water, which had rendered him unhearing as it splashed down into the wash basin; he looked like a bull bowed down to be slaughtered. His paralysed skull, blood-filled and spinning, would not have risen from this attitude of execution, but Řeka's axe did not strike home and the crazed man, groping at the walls, made to depart as if the floors of the manor house were wobbling beneath his feet.

Still inside the bedroom, incapable of deviating from his route alongside the wall, he crashed into the wardrobe and was left wedged between the furniture and the wall. A blast of a kind of idiotic merriment swooped into this cranny.

"Damn, isn't the way clear? Have I not seen the baron, was I not standing behind him? Did I not leave him alive and can I not take whatever I fancy?"

Musing thus on his valour, Řeka, now in no hurry, returned to the picture of the ass treading its path from Samaria to Nazareth. At that moment, the manservant turned off the stream of water rising through the pipes and there was a new sound. The assassin looked up and in a sudden rush opened a drawer just to touch the inside of some object, for it was all too improbable that he was even there.

He took up a fistful of papers and put them back in their place. He fingered the case in which a Browning pistol lay, tossed aside some letter or other, and from the bowels of a portfolio extracted a sheet covered in printing. Thinking to mimic the ways of readers, he held its underside up to the light. An image appeared of the imperial eagle, and when the rays of light no longer passed through the watermark, it vanished. Řeka thought this quite a good game. On his way out, he took the paper with him, along with a seashell glittery enough to appeal to the lunatic.

Having come out into the hallway, Řeka closed the door with all the care he could muster, because he had heard the footsteps of a valet on the floor above, perhaps rushing his way to give him a hiding. The garden was deserted and the twilight grew denser. Řeka made his way back and the axe in his hand was weightless. He walked round the sheds and the cistern, tapping its stone surround, passed several men and then paused by the well as night drew on.

As ten struck, he rose and crossed through the stable in repose.

Images of deeds appear out of the dark of night and are more beautiful than the real thing.

The little donkey has now made it to Nazareth and is lying down on his bundle of straw, the baron is dead and the blood-stained axe is resting on his chest.

Glancing once more at the crescent moon, Řeka recited some crazy poem and, leaving the axe to its fate, took down a rope that was usually used to strap down the restraining bolster on fully laden hay carts.

Having found the loop on one end, he threaded it and tossed it over a beam, waiting now like a frightful fisherman above the bundle of straw that was Hora's bed.

Hora is in his place. He's asleep, his back propped up in the manner of people with a weak heart and his head drooping.

He has not lain down in five years, waiting in a sitting position for the death that now is drawing nigh.

The murderer slipped the noose round, gave the rope a tug and hauled on it with all his might. Hora's head rose barely a span, yet his pitiful frame just did not have the strength to rise to its feet.

CHAPTER FIVE

Hearken to Time and mark it well that you may become wise. Hearken to the night of ages, striding along precipices until cockcrow, and all insouciance shall turn into affliction. The gales have died away and none of the sounds of the countryside is to be heard. The grange retired early and is still abed. The solid rock of the manor house is unstirred, the stables have fallen silent and the servants are still slumbering in their quarters.

Three o'clock struck and Josef looked up from his book. Having failed to find the daystar, he withdrew his head from the oriel in its embrasure and resumed his cogitations.

"Be not of faint heart, rise and make ready to go," he said, which resolve was already the tenth.

Finally, he picked up his cane, knotted his bundle as befitted a pilgrim and, having descended as far as the main gate, came back.

Opening this door was too awkward since, at the first squeak of its hinges, the manor gatekeeper would have come hurrying along to put his weight behind it and make it budge, then, having opened it, he would have bowed to the gentleman sallying forth thus on a whim.

The Reverend Danowitz could not embark on his pilgrimage to Jerusalem without looking silly.

The old baron was asleep, but his retainer stood proud by the threshold, like a pile of broken glass that could only be jumped over with one's cassock hitched up to the bare knees.

Shrinking before both deference and derision, Josef descended to investigate the servants' entrances and, finding these likewise closed, he paused several moments before the doorkeeper's quarters.

Finally, he made up his mind and knocked.

"Give me the key, I want to go out," he told the servant, who was rather casual about his civilities.

Now the need was to return for the cane and the bundle previously made ready, and Josef proceeded like a man in a hurry, though he passed the gatekeeper's little window on tiptoe.

That particular morning, Ouhrov was in no hurry to rise. Josef passed through the village, meeting none but one farmhand and a child. Once out among the fields he paused, no longer apprehensive. The baron slept and the manor house was locked up. Josef could reflect upon his sheer mettle. Upon his nights to come and the sheer distance to Jerusalem.

At the outskirts of the village he was already the pilgrim, having eschewed all the conveniences of the traveller except his cane. He was of course shod, but the scrappy shoes on his feet were so bad that they left him crippled on the very first day. The half-empty pack danced on the priest's back, but there was still hope that the edges of the straps would turn up harness-like and chafe him like the trammels of pilgrims of bygone ages.

On any first day, hopes are at their greenest and miseries commence with a little singing. Well now, our priest, who was trudging along in the certain knowledge that the Ouhrov highway was sufficient of a road to lead proverbially to Rome, may have overlooked certain provisions relative to health. He would fain have trotted past milestones, but the pilgrim's gait has ever been slow and sombre. Thus was his tread more dogged than brisk.

With the cockcrowing village still barely behind him, all that marked him out as a pilgrim was nothing short of oafish. He walked along the bank of the ever-widening river, past the osier beds that alternated now with stony embankments, now with reeds, but the beauty of it all failed to strike even a spark in the priest. His spirits dampened, he dragged his cane behind him, and with his head drooping he looked all too like a penitent des- ...e to expedite his atonement. Eventually the Vltava fell aw... ...ow him as his path began to rise towards some small ele... ...n. A clump of beech trees was growing there and in the... ...t, among some stones, stood a cross. From this omen he ... ...have gone back home, for the hilltop bore a maudlin nam... ...the cross stood on the site of a former gallows. Having p... ...heedless through this part, Danowitz pressed on towa... ...he town of Mirovec, where he paused.

The next day, some dark-eyed ne'er-do-well, who had spent years out on the road, spotted Josef from the thicket where he lurked, and, intrigued by the latter's sagging bag, began to pry: "Where are you going, sir? Unless I'm mistaken, you're the kind of monk that carries a knife with a crooked blade!"

Danowitz offered no reply, and the vagabond, matching his step to the priest's, began to speak at length:

"I'm not offended by your silence, because you can't be thrilled at having me walking with you, any more than I'd enjoy being followed by a bunch of fellows with bags under their arms or on their backs. Quite loath as I am, I can assure you that I'm in no hurry. Having several likings for beer and hard liquors, I can happily bide my time till wherever such lapses come into their own, and I shall accompany you, for I'm sure you'll oblige me."

"That's all well and good," Danowitz replied, "but I have nothing to offer you. I carry neither money, nor wine. What you have mistaken for a bottle is just a linen cloth wound round a stick, like people used to carry. Feel it, you'll find it has no neck."

"Huh!" said the tramp, "You seem exceedingly clear about your impediments! Are you going far? Surely not, or you're going the wrong way about it. Hell, you can't be thinking of spending the nights agreeably at local rectories, can you? I'm sure the benefits of your calling are considerable, so come on, show me. Don't tell me, for God's sake, that the clergy tread the highways with a toothpick between their teeth and their hands behind their backs to signify their hunger!"

Danowitz, who had never stepped outside the world of the priesthood, where all discourse tends to be long-winded, could not be more resolute in his entirely warranted rejection of this brand of chitchat. He did not give the wayfarer the slip and his suppressed rage did eventually shake itself out of his heart. He could have maintained a sullen silence all the way to Jerusalem and, rattling his rosary, he would have really looked like one well versed in the ways of pilgrims. But now it was a wonder that he wasn't sitting with this windbag aboard a fire engine hurtling with its crew the shortest way to the pub. He heard out a list of all dishes made with onions and, being by nature of a glum disposition and a less ravening appetite, confessed that he was suffering.

The men only stopped towards noon.

"What are you intending to do?" Josef asked.

"Let's eat," said the man, "let's eat, sir, and if you're still not hungry, get rid of your afflictions at last. I've heard tell that it's good to tickle the throat with a cock-erel's feather and have a really good retch. Do that, or something else, anything. There's a tavern nearby and by no means the worst."

"Sir," said Danowitz, abashed, for his voluntary penury, which had seemed so desirable at Ouhrov, now looked more like deception or stinginess than Christian virtue, "I've told you I have no money, I shall have to find work from time to time in order to procure such sustenance as I shall need. I have far to go, sir."

"So be it," said the ragamuffin with a barely perceptible smirk, "but on the road a certain courtesy applies, not dissimilar to others. I don't want to ask you where you're bound, what's that to me? But you are going to buy me lunch."

The devout priest's spirit was aggrieved, but the tramp, whose mind was bent solely on getting to the table as fast as possible, persevered with such importunity that Danowitz was too embarrassed to resist.

They set off again, speaking only now and again, for Danowitz found conversation oppressive. He wanted to concentrate on matters that take shape without regard to learning, almost crudely. Foreseeing that he would have to pay the tramp's reckoning at the nearest tavern, for the latter's words brooked no misunderstanding, and unable to countenance the possibility that the whole episode might end with their being harangued by some boorish magistrate, he began to contemplate selling his ring. "I am acutely aware," he mused, turning his bag over, "that my actions have been somewhat reprehensible. I shouldn't have responded to this derelict, nor allowed him to come along with me. He's sturdy enough to fend for himself. Let him do his mischief somewhere else, for goodness' sake!"

Yet on they went. Taverns, those age-old facilities, survive at crossroads to this day. Josef soon spotted the building and the inn sign with its green wreath and felt sure that disaster was imminent.

"Let's go in," said the wayfarer, "let's go on in! This tavern isn't the best we might have found before sundown, but it's away from the village that starts just beyond that bend. That strikes me as an advantage, since the local constable probably doesn't come here for his tripe soup."

They sat down at a table that was more rustic than the tables in real hostelries. Mine host, who had been busying himself in his pens and sheds, followed them inside, alarmed at the whimsical apparel of these travellers.

"This calls for caution, since taverns are still not safe from diners who roam the highways," he thought as he tempered his welcome.

"Right," said the tramp with considerable self-assurance, "give me something to eat, what have you got?"

The publican, maintaining a fairly telling silence, stepped across to an old cupboard leaning against the wall and from under a glass cover took two ripe round cheeses.

"Here you are," he said, setting each one down on a slice of bread. Then he picked up a bottle, filled two shot glasses with brandy and brought them over to the table.

"Is that all?" Danowitz inquired.

"I can't go in for any other fare on a highway travelled by no one. You can see the cheeses are old and, truth to tell, I've been waiting an age to sell at least these two. Once you've paid, I can offer some more since, doubt it not, they are all for sale."

"Today, as it happens," said Danowitz in the lowest tone he could muster, "we have no money, but if you could accept some object instead, I should be greatly obliged to you."

"Well, well," said the publican, "I thought as much, so I can take my food and the drinks back." Despite this assurance, he came up close to the priest to focus his uninhibited attention on his pack.

"All right then," he said, bearing Danowitz's roll of linen away, "I can let you have three sausages each, three cheeses and half a litre of brandy."

"What!" said the tramp, seeing that things had taken a turn for the better, "Do you take us for fools? The linen that you've just bundled away so smartly is worth ten times as much. Give us the full value, man, or treat us to a lunch less frugal. I know what's what and you've hit a brick wall with me."

The publican descended to the cellar to fetch a chunk of meat and Josef departed with his cane and his bag.

The tramp, in whose proximity thievery was a not uncommon occurrence, was not offended by Danowitz's not leaving his bag on the table. He was forbearing with regard to the prudence of friends.

Meanwhile Josef, with no thought of returning, hurried on towards the village. He ran hunched, supporting the bag bobbing on his back with his left hand. Having passed through the village, he turned off the road into a small wood. He was more sorry about the discourtesies that he had suffered for too long than about the lunch or the linen; he was terror-stricken. He had been disconcerted by the unforeseeable practices of the highroad and had finally lost all composure. Unable to proceed and enraged at such skulduggery as merited the severest of penalties, Josef merely sat there in a shallow hollow in the middle of the wood. It was almost evening when, believing that his travelling companion would have left the village by then, he rose and slowly made his way back.

As he reached the first cottages, darkness was already descending. He paused for a moment in thought on the village green, then his shoulders, oddly senescent for his three-and-twenty years, began to rise and shake. Josef was weeping. The gleam of light streaming from the open shop doorway lit up the church tower. So there was a church in the village and the parish priest, beyond all doubt, knew the Danowitz name. Yet Josef was irresolute.

Finally, as if wishing to rip his destiny free of the rights and privileges of aristocracy, while also meaning to thumb his nose at the priesthood, he entered the grocer's shop and, emptying his bag onto the counter, sold all his possessions. Once more he was treated to the inept jibes and fatuities of an oaf who would be unstinting in kissing the backside of the parish priest, but couldn't give a damn for any other priest, especially a poor one.

The black gaps between the trees twinkled with stars; on a night like this it would be possible to walk on till daybreak, but, oh! land, thou art too far! Thou art too near, land! Land of roughnecks, yokels and vagabonds who all live their lives simply and with no misgivings, while pilgrim clerics are left to seek refuge in oak woods.

Having set forth from the village where he had sold his ring and all the things he had brought with him from Ouhrov, Josef reached the hamlet of Louňovice in the dead of night. He sought out the inn and, bedding down as snugly as possible, he slept.

He slept through till daybreak and woke craving, without a single qualm, a spot of tea and a breakfast of eggs, toast and butter.

"I need to come by some small remuneration to show that money matters are of little moment," he thought as he ordered his food, which he consumed in no time and without further thought.

Nevertheless, Josef came out of the inn still wearing the fairly unmistakable aspect of a wayfarer; his legs, evidently in poor shape, struggled forward, squelching mud along the edges of his soles. Water squirted up from beneath his shoes and his outlandish overcoat got soaked through, for it had begun to rain.

"Could you tell me, sir, how far it is to the main road that leads to Tábor and Vienna?" Danowitz asked a man who was about to start mowing.

"What?" said the mower, bereft of laughter or at least the vocalising of it, for he was laughing with flaps of his hand and the silent convulsions of a kind of gleeful wonderment. "Oo, oo!" he eventually spluttered, pointing at the priest, who had no option but to flee.

"To hell with such dunderheads," said the priest, making his scorn more callous than it actually was.

Next day, as he made his way along the Tábor highroad, Danowitz ate and drank at wayside inns in exactly the manner of commercial travellers. He had enough money to go for four weeks without knowing hunger, though that time was too short, for whoever could make it to Palestine on foot in just one month? And then, on any journey even the full-bellied and well-shod suffer, since nights are as cold as the mountain heights and torrid days burn in the balefire of the sun.

Amid the din of harvest time, which was just starting in the uplands, amid the blare of barrel organs and among the vineyards of southern Moravia, Danowitz dwelt in a severe and solitary world of his own. Buffeted by the world, battered and bruised, derided, he was like a fairground figure whose behind has been laid bare. Frazzled, his feet worn to shreds and his heels leeching blood, how could he still be contemplating a journey to Jerusalem? He sat down on a bank and his overheated brain shifted about in the middle of his skull like a snail inside its shell. There were tears aplenty on this jaunt!

"Now here's a mystery," he said faced with a revelation inscribed in the pages of the weather lore of travel. "Why does the glaring truth elude me when its radiation is breathing in my face?"

"Sir," said a puny road mender, "you must not confuse two quite different things: it is disgraceful to hear you railing at the want of a reply to your Christian greeting. Forget it, if you're that prideful, I couldn't give a damn for the honour, but as sure as I have this shovel in my hand, you pipsqueak, I can tan your hide for you. Note well that you can only win your case if we talk!"

Josef's rather crackpot Christianity subsided into an unfamiliar tract of his heart. Hearing the discourse of filthy hostelries and the things spouted at forks in the road, proceeding with rectitude in his scruffy boots amid such utter, jocund vulgarity as had not been seen in the cavernous interiors of church and library since the middle ages, Danowitz rested his weight on his cane, which was an ordinary wooden stick again.

The drawbacks of having traded in his effects began to dawn and he would have returned to retrieve his bag if it had not been too far back. Jerusalem was forgotten and humility was forgotten.

Loath to return to Ouhrov, for the old baron would surely have scoffed at his pilgrimic pursuit, Josef turned east. "Dressed like this," he thought, "I can't set foot in Vienna, but there's no reason why I shouldn't go to my Istęba estate in Poland."

Having reached the borders of Galicia, Josef now resembled all Josefs who tramp the highroads. He might still have been barely familiar with the ways of real men and he had no idea how to secure lunch amid fields filled with game, but he did have some inkling of taverns. To an innkeeper toying with a kitchen knife to show how unafraid he was he could chat with a demeanour that no one could have considered apprehensive. He could look back at wenches squishing about on a threshing floor, and he would have wished them a good day and a good night, though for now his apparel was still too conspicuous. Too often beyond the notional frontier did those relentlessly pesky breasts and thighs catch the eye and a bygone rapture began to reanimate its age-worn countenance.

Danowitz was like a renegade priest dashing between gambling den and tryst. His head was filled with some locution that he meant to utter at a particularly opportune moment, but his hardihood went no further than the intention. As he passed one lass, who was standing most beguilingly over a washboard, he re-found his momentarily forgotten youthful exuberance and could not resist looking back at her.

At the Przegonina crossroads he came upon a carriage heading in the same direction.

"Good day," he said, stepping round to the front, and the yokel, whose mare had just put her best foot forward, had ample time not to reply with a single sentence.

"Where are you going?" he did ask eventually, leaning out of the wickerwork body of his britzka. "Wolonce, you say? Well, why go there on foot? I can take you right to the middle of the village."

Josef climbed aboard. A few rocky moments sufficed to dismiss all uncertainty as to this kindly driver's inebriated condition. Luckily, he didn't fall off and the conveyance moved on in a laborious exhilaration.

"Sir," the peasant began as he gradually took in all the obscured clues to Danowitz's station, "there are two ways to travel: on horseback or barefoot. What man are you, not to have chosen either the one or the other?"

"Ah," Josef replied, in a Polish mangled like the Slovak of politicians of later times, "that rule of passage doubtless has its exceptions."

"For sure, exception is the master of every rule, but who can make head or tail of the ways lawyers express things?" said the peasant. "Being too honest to grapple with the damned tyranny of the bailiffs, I've been completely done for by the prerogatives of distillers as guaranteed them by the law. Just have a sniff of this sea," he said, raising his nose and exhaling the malodour of hard liquor, "that's your Polish ocean! Have a drink, sir, or, if you will, let's sing a song!"

"A squadron of uhlans smashed a squadron of hussars. We live in abundance and our fortune is too much to manage. Hurrah, hurrah, hurrah!"

"The neck of this bottle's too narrow," said Danowitz.

"Seek not to amend the old ways," replied the drunkard, "seek not to amend the old ways or we might have a falling out. Are sips to be separated by tongue or throat? Consider well this unimpeachable local pursuit not as a foreigner, but as a fellow whom I have invited aboard my britzka!"

Danowitz drank and voiced his gratitude under constraint. Fortunately, the contemptuous gesture with which he returned the bottle passed unobserved and its scrupulosity ensured no harm was done.

He drank again, and again preparing the expanse of his mind for something to say or sing that would strike home, he drank, his fist ready to strike.

"What gave you that idea?" Danowitz asked, now unconstrained, "why do you think that?"

And with a flick of his whip the peasant hollered by way of reply: "Heigh-ho! Heigh-ho!"

The horse, after the manner of all draught animals who have few occasions for going wild, broke into a gallop so furious that it would have stunned even the boiler smith who had sold it because of its craziness. That evening Josef was finding the expanses of the universe somewhat vaster than normal, and when the drunken coachman collapsed into his corner, he took the unwarranted crush badly amiss.

"Get off me," he said, "are you totally drunk?"

A bloodshot eye turned on Danowitz.

"Get off," Josef yelped, suddenly sober. But a blow was struck and now he keeled over and toppled. A cloud of sparks and dark accompanied his fall. As he lay face-down in the dust, the other careered off, shouting and brandishing his whip.

After a moment Danowitz rose to his feet, stepped off the roadway and sat down on a boulder. He spat blood from his now missing teeth, while swellings made his features comical.

Time passed and night was drawing nigh, a night no less painful and no less accursed than nights at Ouhrov.

Hearken to the dark of ages, striding along precipices until cockcrow. On these plains and mountain chains of night all insouciance shall turn into affliction, for the solid rock of the manor house is still unstirred.

When Danowitz rose and stepped back onto the road, gathering up no part of his pilgrim's paraphernalia. Turning round, he walked to a village quite other than whither his steps had been bent. He sought out the Jewish ferryman, then travelled the three days to Istęba like a baron meaning to catch his steward unawares.

CHAPTER SIX

Matters long heralded were drawing towards their conclusion, for no one can conceal a fire beneath their coat and no one can hide a glowing coal within their clenched fist.

For some considerable time you trained in the disciplines of war, you harnessed horses and charged into the fray until Hungary was free of the enemy. You heralded this moment which was imminent and everyone knew that it would come to pass.

Regiments blue and red, dreary barracks, and a stable block spilling over with thwarted galloping will take their stand with colours flying, and before they pull out onto the blood-soaked highway and the broad tracts of battles to be fought, bands will strike up on the square.

A stupid journalist, thrice to be transformed before being granted the indulgence of death with a direct hit, trumpets and rings out, proclaims, announces and spreads the word about some death or other that is of concern to no one and over which not even the Emperor weeps.

A piece of chaff consumed by fire, and a name paltry and unknown, forgotten along with its agnomen in the hour of death. The name of one who hankered after the glory and the power that had passed him by.

The name of a man of no account, and a demise undeserved. An undeserved demise, a tiny item repeated, alas, so often in the dailies. A tiny sigh heaved and a moment lingered over a misadventure so far, far away.

Where is Sarajevo, where is that country?

A pious duke, being borne hither and thither in his fine carriage, was killed at the country's heart by a young man who, in that same instant, also destroyed himself.

A pity about those deaths – twice the pity! The waste of each body and a waste of energy. Shall the hands of the assassins reloading their weapons be cut short, have the caution and the admonition issued to the avengers been enough? There is no power equal to liberation from these, such ancient wrongs, and as yet the red of the flag is vacuous.

As yet, the red of the flag is vacuous.

The cities of Germany are in uproar and supine Bohemia has yet to make up its mind. War will usher in a darkness that will last for three years.

Meanwhile, men are packing the knapsacks that they will lug with them to army barracks, and the rage and the fury melt away into a whingeing that will fall silent in the wide open spaces.

This silence will be accursed, for of all things it most resembles fear.

Ranting posters and the deplorable image of a poor fellow praying for his army and whooping for war did stir these parts. As they entered the gates of a monstrous slaughterhouse and an age of carnage, some raved their acclamation, some screamed after the spoils of war, others went irresolute and yet others got drunk, though not blending their zeal with wine. For this was a time of hard liquor.

Outside the tavern, evening is descending, perhaps sombre enough for me to remain seated at my table, for wine cheereth the heart. For wine is free.

Five hussars, who had been accorded some consequence by the war, raised their re-filled glasses and they raised their voices: "May the green grass grow! May the bastard who spoiled our fun be made to milk a bull!"

A somewhat senescent gentleman, who had gone a bit crackers with the moon in the ascendant or merely with some fine feeling, leaned across the table top, knocking over his wine, and spouted some quite resolute and spirited homily, though the general insobriety had risen substantially and no one could appreciate it quite as it merited.

"Cut the cackle, you pimple," said young František, whose nickname at the barracks was Curry-comb, though, unable to decline their kind invitation, he had been drinking equally from this troublemaker's glass as from the others'. One poor fellow, almost half-dead, whom in an act of high-minded and charming playfulness they'd pushed down and crammed underneath the bench, bellowed, threatening to cut the throat of anyone who laid a finger on him. Just then, the band that had been bashing the drinkers' ears hit its stride and started scraping away at their instruments with ten times the vigour.

"Do me the honour of accompanying me upstairs," said a soldier amid the knot of men pushing and shoving in front of some girl.

The music, drowning out his voice and winging it away after its own manner, might almost have saved him, but girls of this kind are attuned to the ways and graces of men enough to know all about invitations that they haven't even heard right.

"All right," she replied, elbowing her way through the pack, "come on, monkey."

He made to put an arm around her waist. She was about to lean against his shoulder and they, already shaking their backsides in anticipation, might have made a decorous exit without causing trouble. Except that one tiny hussar, who until then had stuck close to his pals, burping and puking quite opportunely in random places and against a background of ordinary small talk, suddenly went slightly wild.

"Sit down," he said and went up to the lover elect, "damn it, man, sit down or I'll knock the living daylights out of you."

"What?" said the infantryman, brandishing a fist, for he knew all about brawling.

Clearly, František had parted company with his good sense and, driven on by venom, had delivered a vicious insult, since his dapper opponent seemed neither feeble enough, nor drunk enough for little František to trounce him. The man rose to his feet and Curry-comb, fumbling for some telling byword in a foreign tongue, landed his first blow on the man's calf.

The girl squealed as if it were not better to leave all such excesses to the obtuse and, in an orderly manner, take some other to her bed.

At this tavern, things had deviated long before from their customary cast. The tables were like animals and should anyone reach for the vessel containing his wine, he would not find it in its place.

"Oh bother," said Kateřina, now ignoring the skirmish, although the soldier's fine ear had almost been ripped off, "why did he have to go poking his nose into things that are no business of his? I was making for the hussars when he just got in the way."

Beyond all expectation, František was putting up quite a good fight, but although he was valiant and Kateřina's interest was turning his way, he would have come off worst if the other four hussars had not settled the wrangle differently.

"Come now," said the gentleman, who believed he might speak, having spent fifty florins or more on wine, "come now, do you really need this? Soldiers in the same army! On the eve of a great war! Shame on you for bringing the sword of which you have been given custody into alehouse brawls!"

"We're the soldiers here, we're the soldiers, for God's sake!" said one of the hussars, hinting that he would not suffer anyone else to go ploughing their furrow.

Someone thumped his fist on the table and the bang was the signal for six soldiers to smash the place up. The defender of good manners, reciprocity and the helping hand, qualities that should be present in armies not just in times of peril, was given a hiding. He left his sleeve in the grip of an infantryman who should have been extolling rather than drubbing him, and having been dumped outside, he set off to find a policeman, sucking on a cut and spitting out a quantity of blood as he went.

Harmony returned to the tavern, smashed up only in part. There *is* a war on. The gentle purring of the noble rule of law has been drowned out by the commotion, and every man jack has, driven by his particular dread, inferred that anything goes.

Let no holds be barred, let drinks be drunk, since the drinks are free today and for the last time.

Whores no longer fuss about stockings and madams weep in the lobbies of brothels.

There's little music in Buda. Everything is out of joint, everything is changing. This disreputable tavern is an argosy and the wine a solace-filled sea.

"Give me a tankard!"

"I want that tart back!"

The night was too long and the door was open; enter several drunks for whom there was no room left. No matter what language they spoke.

"We don't give a damn, we're just fine. There's only one who turns me on, that scruffy tart's the one I want. Keep knocking it back, you fool, you don't know what's coming!"

They told some creaky, quite hoary old joke for the umpteenth time. They kept grinding out the same old song, regardless, as a shift for heartache, a shift for these poor wretches' farewells.

They still had time. The night wasn't over yet. Having fun, heedless, lost in the din and disorder, a herd of loners who, undaunted by barracks, by the name of army and host, shrieked cheek by jowl in their private wasteland. None of them knew the next one. Each was alone, thumbing and kneading his dread, each in his own silence, which the din of taverns cannot engulf.

Rolling hills of Ouhrov, pastures and woodlands of the Carpathians and you, scorching street filled with voices, I'm bringing my tale to an end, strike me down right here and now! Down to the bottom of a bottle drunk dry, down into the lap of the most shameless of whores!

"What's that, that weird noise?" said František, raising his head from the embrace of his hands.

"That? Nothing! The drumbeat of a company departing."

"Come on!" they responded, "stuff this dozy barman! Are you going to squat here till daylight, supping gnat's piss in this dump?"

The street was sinking into darkness, a herd, a host of men, slowing down at every turn, disappeared round each bend to reappear like running water. From somewhere or other came echoes of the weepy sound of violins and the intermittent bleating of a drunk.

"You and my brother," said František, raising his inebriated face to the shoulder of Jakub, his fellow-soldier from Ouhrov, "you are two I shall remember."

"Honestly," the latter replied, "I'm going to regret knowing you, you poor little sod, what d'you want? Where's the rush?" And grabbing his hand, he twisted his wrist.

This Jakub, whose very grossness precluded all idea of fellow feeling or sentiment, was glad of the hustle and bustle that was taking shape. He'd missed out on any luck as a man in his days at Ouhrov, and Buda, with all its particular cant that needed to be known, a city of a dandyesque complexion and verbal skirmishing, was also proving somewhat disappointing. The ineradicable mark of the daredevilry that can, after all, spring from any inner being, evident in a constant readiness for confrontations and freak events where strength still counts for something, this proclivity, manifest only in moments of folly, might now have brought him the great distinctions and a kind of glory of which he had heard tell.

"See," he said, pointing to a group of decent fellows from somewhere in Hungary, who even when they're blind drunk are not entirely heedless of their hussars, "see how they're gawking at us! Christ, let's go and make mincemeat of the bloody Serbs. Whoopee!"

The bunch of ne'er-do-wells, undoubtedly no more resolute than Jakub, whooped their enthusiasm in return. Someone started to sing and the street broke into uproar as if on command.

Next came odd foretastes of a war where even the craven can be victorious.

One abject, big-bellied advocate, whose shrew of a wife would, on a whim, hound him, brandishing her duster, all round their well-enclosed property, almost resembled a hero. Following behind the soldiers, he could hear the sound of drumming coming from the vast arena of a grim field, he could hear the whizz of bullets bouncing off armoured shelters, he could hear carbines and the charging of howitzers, but standing in the midst of this tempest, all the endless flashing of thunderbolts, he resembled the fabled cannoneer Jabůrek. Surfacing from his reveries, this gullet on two legs might have given the entire military some pretty earthy encouragement. He sang away in the midst of the pack, which did bear him some resemblance, given that such bloody-arsed chicken livers are more numerous than is fitting.

František, lacking Jakub's mettle and being way more stupid than he even appeared, might very well have wept, though such behaviour would have been too simple and František did so want to be taken for a hussar, though it was only his weapon that made him one. Three years' service with the regiment is sufficient to confuse such a sluggish spirit, and a proper war was calculated to paralyse him just as it did whole hosts.

The rankling finally passed, he was almost sober now as he walked on, and having recalled his orders, he quickened his pace. He wanted to be in the thick of his squadron, discerning a feeble and forlorn beauty in obedience and in an army going on the march.

Having arrived, he began to undress, mindful of all these things, and because this was war, he hung his hussar's sabre in a prominent place.

Jakub wrote a letter to Ouhrov full of braggadocio, wrestling with his drunken state as he finished it off.

"What are you lot up to," he said to the soldiers still sitting around on their bunks, drinking straight from bottles, "what are you up to, can't you do anything at the proper time? You're supposed to be asleep by now! If an officer spots us with a light on, it's me who'll get it in the neck. And anyway, what if we're moving out tomorrow!"

"Keep your shirt on," they replied, "don't you know that a weary horse catches up fastest?"

This soldier thought too kindly of his friends, who had no wish to fight for any of the Emperor's causes, or for the marketplace, or for trading opportunities worldwide.

Having sealed the envelope and written on it the postmaster's name, Jakub added the words: "Pass this on to Josef Jakub at the grange."

Then he rose and, holding fast to all his soldierly assertiveness, he doused the lamp.

Outside, dawn was breaking. The world was not standing still and these portentous matters could neither draw even half a veil across the moon, nor retard the rising of the sun. Knots of people, hungry for news, stood reading the daily papers. In a thousand places the same sorry joke was told and inept hoarders chased after every bit of small change to squirrel it away in their coffers.

It was the twenty-fifth of July and negotiations were not yet at an end. *Vorwärts* was still speaking out against war and a whirlwind of despatches made known the perfidious positions of governments.

Meanwhile, however, troops were already assembling on the borders of empires. Envoys had had plenty of time to exchange courtesies. Baron Geisl, Tschirschky

and all the others who'd had four years during which to camouflage their aptitude for buffoonery.

The dignity of dominions, that inanity put on hold whenever there is the chance of a spot of pillage, an inanity lifted from the refuse heaps of time, had had its sparkle restored and a sickly Europe was bestriding her mare.

Gone was the pinch of prudence proper to trades and business dealings. Gone was any residue of regret, for spadroon, standard and mitrailleuse had become words of poetry and happenstance.

The twaddle of negotiators and the hatching of wars that are always about money. The foul and obscene fraudulence and ultimately the fighting, the surge of fears and of heroism so long kept hidden.

If only there were no zealous and perfervid hand to bare the blade and raise the standard high!

If only there were none of that timeworn and terrible obedience to the bugle call! Thousands, and thousands more, poor souls advancing in bulging capes. Oh, the excitements of schools and stories told and books! Oh, the games and heroic expeditions! Oh, the tears and empathy dispensed to no one until this day!

To the sound of the drum I onward go, hurrah, hurrah, let's thrash the foe!

The men had made a kind of compact with the horrors that were imminent, through them they were to win renown, they were to thrive on blood, as a plant thrives on water. None was angry and none wished to kill people, but torn away from his rabbit-like existence and with his coat tails hitched up and one hand raised, the defender of widows and orphans had made it all the way to the Serbian frontier or to Horodenka, and behind a barrier of *Feldgendarmes* he would be firing from very fear.

Meanwhile the vast precincts of barracks were filling up with soldiers, and children's playgrounds, Jockey Club riding halls, showgrounds, the Capuchin orchard and palace courtyards were full of tents. The railways brought them in by the hundred and by the thousand, the soldiers lying on the carriage floors. Then it was that women brisker than she-eagles dashed about in the night, others took charge of the kitchens and served food, and yet others, clad from top to toe in white, flocked to the still empty field hospitals. Suffice it for some officer to step forward and say that his men are hungry, let him tinker with his binoculars amid the hideous jennies and they'll all go crazy and fetch their entire larder.

These do-gooders and these urban spinsters have not been praised nearly enough, although they did a lot of weeping and they picked plenty of roses.

The affairs of war gathered pace. On August 1st, a Saturday, France mobilised, Germany declared war on

Russia, and the British navy, assembled at Portland, went on a war footing. The next day, German airships sailed out over French territory and bombs landed on Lunéville.

The war was beginning.

That notwithstanding, the flustered babbling of envoys did not slacken for four days, until Emmich's army began their march across Belgian territory and troops from Hannover and Westphalia sallied forth from Aix-la-Chapelle.

Regrettably, in no army was there a Napoleon to lend some wit to the carnage. *Jeder Stoß ein Franzos! Zum Frühstück auf nach Paris!* – such gibbering by belly-worshippers and the puffing and panting of accordions, that was the voice of the troops. They were to be annihilated and dispersed like the dust of highways, not, unfortunately, for their scurrility, but for their fortitude.

The hussars of Buda, suddenly unhorsed, were crammed into railway carriages. The train's progress was slow. There was an enforced wait at every station, because the way ahead was blocked.

"Get your cards out," said Jakub, and some windbag, who, quite improbably, also hailed from Ouhrov village, replied:

"That's a lousy way to kill time. I knew a chap who was dead keen on it, he'd play on market days, and even with the bride at weddings. I could tell you quite a tale about the good it did him. He got such a beating that he never recovered."

"That's as may be," they told him, "but keep your babble to yourself." A soldier, tormented by the sheer mass of food that had come his way at each stop, went to sit closer to the door, because his queasiness was mounting.

"Mind you don't throw up your watch," said František, finding some comfort in the distress of others.

Finally someone opened his bag and cards found their way into the players' hands.

"Cut!"

"Play!" said Jakub, opening the game.

"I'd like to know," said František to no one in particular, "where we're going."

"That's neither here nor there," a voice in the corner replied, "they fire the same bullets everywhere."

"We're headed for Galicia. Everybody knows that, it's how it is."

They wound up their game.

"Stuff your bloody cards, will you, and let me sleep."

Jakub, who'd been so keen on playing, slithered down under his blanket. "It's night," he said.

It was their third day on the train. They were tired of stations full of waiting and soldiers. No alighting. No drinking. The hospitable ladies with their plates and tea cans had vanished. Another evening was coming.

A station pillar, forming with its shadow an open fork all day long, was now closing up.

"I'd like to know when this trip'll be over," said František, but no one offered a reply.

A soldier came in with a lamp, which he hung in the middle of the carriage, and said: "Lights out one hour from now. Good night." He was treated to the most vulgar of responses, then came back.

"You watch it, mate, or I'll give you a clip round the ear!"

"Me!" said the hussar, looming into the smoky half-light of the lamp. "I'd think twice if I were you, you jack-a-dandy!"

Five or ten arguments begun ended in a hush. Jakub yawned in his corner. "I want to sleep, budge up a bit."

Half-way through the night a voice rang out, though no one paid it any attention. Silence reigned. An officer was running along the line of carriages, glancing inside at the doors.

"Anybody missing?"

Propped up on his elbow, as on a battlefield, Jakub replied: "No, sir."

"Good, we're moving off."

But an hour passed, and another, and a third and their train was still firmly wedged in the dark, or forgotten.

The night was like a castle that was about to be captured, though sleep was still possible within its chambers. The distribution of firepower had yet to reach the Carpathian chain, so hunger and the rough seas of battle were reassuringly remote.

How merciful, how soothing this tarrying was. How much better an hour spent cramped and snoring in crannies inside a carriage, or between the heads of horses, than the broad daylight of Galicia. You will traverse fairly barren roads, without finding any worse spot to sleep. Ahead lies a wait that will end only years from now. Ahead lies a wait that will be broken only by death. Ahead lies a wait that will end only when the empire dies of the military glory to which you are pledged. You will have gone from nation to a nation's dregs, from depth to depth, from war to war before you can return. For now, may this night stand still, may it be prolonged until twilight. May the morning star expire at the moment of its rising, and may the blazing firmament be made dark!

Ah, the lull has had its day and the bugle's voice is broken into a thousand piercing tones.

Arise, the time has come!

Give the terrified horses their fodder! Wake up!

Not even this day is the last and as you slept the cataclysm has barely drawn nearer.

Came the sixth day of the journey. Nagy, a hussar who'd been dreaming of his native Gyula, woke and began to write a letter home, for his thinking brooked no delay.

"We've turned north," he wrote, "and having crossed the mountains we're nearing the empire's borderlands. It's as horrible as mid-November, and this morning we found every object covered in hoarfrost."

They all beat the writer to breakfast and his portion was smaller than the others'. Poor fellow, if he'd torn up his barely finished letter, he'd have written another, far sadder, because the indignity of having someone else eat his breakfast left him shattered. Once more he was the little apprentice, wide-eyed in the workshop and dreaming of Gyula, as his master takes his repast.

František, now back from the horse trucks, had sat down on a wooden ledge and was going through his things.

"This buckle's no use to me," he said, setting aside the clasp, ornate enough to have no appeal even for a hussar. "Do you fancy buying a pretty neat buckle?" he asked Jakub.

"Man," he replied, "did you steal it or did they throw it in when you were buying neatsfoot oil for your tack in Gyula?"

František was uncomprehending, but Jakub pounced on the bauble and hurled it as far as he could. František was furious and the hussars had something to laugh at.

"Silence!" bellowed the corporal who was dashing from carriage to carriage with an order of some kind.

"When are we leaving, sir?"

"Right now," he replied, "the track's clear, be ready for off."

Finally, around midday, the train began to move. Two or three hussars started singing again.

"Stop fooling about," said Jakub, "Lift not up your horns!"

The train had crossed the watershed and now followed rivers that dropped towards the plains of Galicia. This region would be churned up and turned into a barren wasteland, war would burn bright as fire and villages were to become dens of thunder. There would be famine. Peasant hands are idle and farmers' horses follow behind the soldiers with cartloads of ammunition. Blow ye the trumpet and add ye the tumult of drumbeats! Whatsoever liveth wheresoever, let it flee! The forests are catching fire, and in the villages not one stone has been left on another, there are cisterns of blood on the fields of savagery and the standards of armies are upraised like the unicorn's horn.

CHAPTER SEVEN

The rye had all been cut and threshed and the ears collected in the fields. The time was approaching when past harvests no longer needed to be eked out, and the late summer, with its abundance of lavish parish feasts, was drawing nigh.

Farmers dwell in security and eat their fill at this time, when storms will no longer burn up their profits and nothing will give them a fright.

There may be talk of some war, but such talk is nothing new and comes back every summer at eventide.

Rumours of a great war have been rife for ten years. Whether of a callow youthfulness or advanced in years, men will go forth, and the ferocious countenance of the army will turn against the foe, who will throng to towns and cities and across frontier rivers.

For many a long year, story-telling has been the tithe on harvests, sought by none, but if some old sweat comes out with something in a yard full of people, as is apt to happen precisely on a Saturday, they will take up his words and start shouting them about until it all swells into an ominous siren wail.

Beside a tranquil pond at which oxen drink, people are apt to speak of the blood that pours from the wounds of fighting men. The latest terrifying fiction flares up, burning as a sacrificial offering to the war that is already drawing nigh.

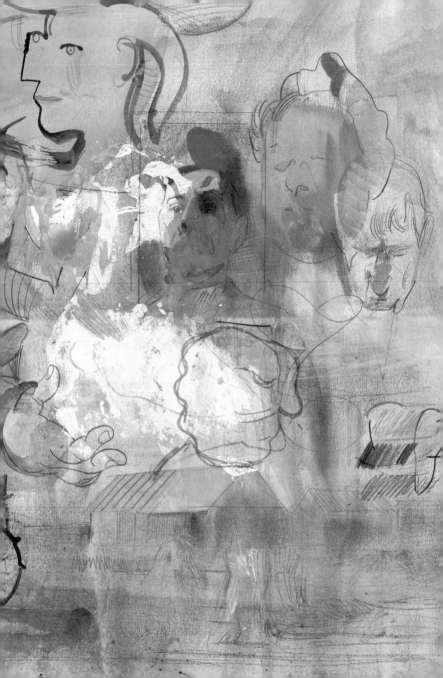

I'll take some flour and hide it, since I know what florins used to be worth in times of war.

The flesh of this narrative was still lodged in the narrator's teeth when he forgot all about his circumspection, and his doubts stilled when the morrow brought another working day. On that day, after all the prophesying, an ordinance of mobilisation did land, like a lightning flash to be followed by the rumble of thunder, right in their midst. Rampant mystifications born of benightedness and asininity were fit to set the entire grange in a frenzy. Řeka, Ber, Jakub and all those who reiterated the Emperor's summons were buffeted by the gale. All the creepy hands of ignorance came groping after these crazy individuals. An eternity of penury had almost made skeletons of them. Blood had already been spilled and bone marrow frozen. For years they had heard naught but the rattle of chains and the tread of the beast plodding ahead of them. The Emperor's address, majestic and well-constructed, an address that stripped their limbs of their last tatters, was for them!

Jakub read it out and they listened to it over and over again.

Řeka was overtaken by a frightful fascination. Had he not touched the body of a hanged man, had he not beheld the stillness and the calm that had finally ensued? The body had hung like a plumb bob, the head appearing to listen and the wide eyes turning no way.

What a way for a war to start!

He was a Serb and I dressed him in a shroud.

There's nothing simpler, there is nothing simpler than war!

"It's obvious," said Ber, thinking of the man who'd killed the duke, "it's obvious he'll be tortured to death and made a martyr of. The Emperor will have him put down."

They spoke of all kinds of murders, though Hora's corpse had left them unmoved.

That case of suicide, since who would have gone to the trouble of murdering a poor fellow who had no more than the twenty-crown coin left stitched into his bag? That suicide, so understandable, could have been neither a portent, nor anything else. Despite the words of the ox handler, the hanging body was not of their world. Events had passed this killing by and run ahead. They'd taken the weight of the dead man and Ber had removed the noose. Then they'd laid the body down on the floor of the entryway.

That morning, work was delayed somewhat, with the workmen held up, chatting in huddles about what Hora had been.

Obtuseness has its rights, but kindliness outranks them. So they did pay him some small tribute and let the stinginess be his prerogative.

"He kept a good look-out from the coach-box when he was driving horses."

"He used to drive foals. Ah, those were the days! I'm sure he'd happily go through that business 'in my second year in service' again. I'm sure he'd act no differently if he were enlisting today."

That was all that could be said. They'd placed a neckerchief over his face and shaded the window.

The dead man, his tongue stuck out half-way and his legs bent, had resembled a gruesome, sneering dummy, but he was accorded some peace and dignity. Someone's betrothed prepared a linen sheet. Ber fetched a candle and lit it. They bound up the old wound on his knee and raised his head.

A noblesse as ancient as human labour, the bond that endures among labourers, lent the storeroom all the dignity due. A heedful universe stood outside the door.

At least for a moment, Řeka took part in this act of mercy, though such belated justice could only be in vain, the killer having failed to confess or come to his senses. The workmen rose from their task and the beauty of it drifted away or became invisible. War was pressing.

"Get going, don't hold up the harvest! Jump to it! Stop loitering!"

The terms of the call to arms brooked no delay.

Several of the young lads got their boxes ready.

"Where am I to get hold of a blanket, like it says in the order? How can I show up in threadbare trousers?"

In all the hustle and bustle, charity, so inarticulate, could say nothing. Would it count as an act of mercy that Řeka gave his bedding away?

Would it count as a good deed that young Novák jammed his nearly new boots on his dad's terrible feet?

Here are some foot wraps and a neck scarf! Of course, the wedding skirt is in two pieces, but what of it. Take whatever you need. Take some bread and a spoon and a knife. It can't be helped, take some duck down and all the money. The womenfolk raise their arms heavenwards; they weep, but this downpour is no tempest.

In every province there was great sorrowing, but such things are naught. Those not fired up by clarion call, drumbeat, banners and the tolling of bells went crazy and compelled their very poverty to cough up the money. These magnificent dullards paid out far in excess of their means. They had to spend their last and run up debts with Lei, who, by some miracle, stocked everything from lamps to bayonets.

A wife whose fidelity had always been in doubt wrung her hands as she got together a hundred knickknacks to go in her husband's kitbag. "Have these safety pins, a needle and thread, buttons, a pencil and some paper."

But her husband, still hung over from the night before, tipped the things out onto the floor. "Cut the fuss, you tart," he replied, finding greater consolation in his own cursing than in her attentiveness. "Keep your stuff and I hope I never come back to this dump!"

But not even the cussing could hold her back.

"Here's a little bowl, some grease and a valet's gloves; you might find a use for them."

She was being the sister of mercy notwithstanding her wicked secret.

A wind of demented zeal was blowing across every land, and the old baron made enough hay wains available, for he, too, had to do something for the motherland. The men couldn't make it to them fast enough. Each decked out after his own manner, they clambered over the rails with their bulging packs.

Good bye! Good bye! Good bye!

Shed tears around the wagons, give voice to your lament, for silence is more ill-humoured than tears.

If you'd been expecting anything other than my leaving, I wouldn't have gone. If you'd said the regiment's bugle call was the trumpeting of a swashbuckler I wouldn't have obeyed the summons.

With the screaming and the weeping, the adulation and the sheer damned doggedness with which you rustle up togs fit for a winter encampment you have suppressed the voice of revolt and the urge to rebel that lurks in every man. You let the men drink more than at other times, you put your arms around them and called them by their first names. One last time, Johnny! You yourselves stuck a service cap on each man's head. Sadists! Gawping onlookers, their hearts seizing up with sympathy, but unable to deny themselves the dismal spectacle. Play-actors who have taken a liking to this tragic drama, this self-abuse, this almost voluntary status of a pawn. Stay! Have your fill of ashes! The soldier with the ginger moustache, the one you saw off with such pomp, will return to drum a measure of reason and devotion into you.

One wagon, wearing the aspect lent it by those seeing the men on their way, returned their good-byes but scantly as it moved off. One man did wave back, one leaned out, but the handkerchief he shook open could rise to no more than a limp flutter. All went quiet.

Some who fancied following the wagons broke off from the knot of people left standing at the edge of the village. But they came back having gone only part-way.

Ouhrov now had plenty of time for rumination.

"If the Russians launched a proper attack, they could reach Bohemia in five days," said Ber.

"How could they get through the imperial army?"

"Pah!" he retorted, "you don't know Russia, it's so very big and so very powerful. If they get this far, I'll guide them to Hradec by the shortest route. Yes," he repeated to the doubters, who were amazed by his blaspheming, "I'll guide them by the shortest route. What do I care about decrees from the Austrian Emperor and authorities that are only ever German? I know the Russians and I know what I'm talking about. If the whole of Russia went to war, no one could stand up to them, given the country's twice the size of China."

Jakub shrugged. "Maybe," he said. "What I'm wondering is how we'll harvest the oats, because these men won't be back anytime soon."

"You can leave the fields to themselves, who's going to hang around here now with a war like this under way! I reckon we'll all be going, you too, Ber, because this time they're not going to be choosy over who they enlist."

"Stop talking rubbish," Ber replied, "I'm sixty."

"Yes, but you haven't got kids."

"I've got a son in the army," said Jakub, weighing the benefits of his parenthood with a measure of uncertainly. "So much the worse," he said after a moment's thought, "because what'll I do if he doesn't come back?"

They reached the barn with its bristling thatch across which flashed the shadow of a flock of pigeons. Ten o'clock struck. This Friday was all too like a Sunday, with everybody walking about hands in pockets. The boiler attendant had left and the engineer declined to put in an appearance. The estate manager had joined his regiment and the only steward left was Čapek.

"This year's harvesting," said Ber, wallowing in the accumulating disasters, "is going to take until St Catherine's Day and the oats will get buried under snow."

Outside his inn, Lei was tidying into boxes the shoddy nosegays intended as buttonholes for the new recruits.

"Well, well," said Jakub as they passed, "you've got quite a few left. But of course, man, who'd buy anything so ridiculous on his way to the battlefield. This war's not remotely like life in the barracks at Hradec."

"If you're not buying, leave them alone," said Lei, "and anyway, I don't like ragamuffins hanging about outside my place. Be on your way or come inside."

"Well, my friends, shall we?"

Ber, however, was already heading inside. They drank spirits, saying little. Ber was spinning various impieties. "This war," he ended, "is for the destruction of all mankind. Life's been too good and people have been breeding like locusts. So, hasn't the war come at just the right moment?"

"Might have, or might not," they replied, "let's see how it ends." The day drew on. At this hour the fire in every stove was dying down and cooks stood destitute over their pots. But this day no one will be coming in for supper, no one will be back before nightfall and no one will give a thought to their work. The old shoes and rags in which the women had pottered around all the day before were left on the floor. Dishes went unwashed and a washtub full of grunge stood stinking by the door.

"Oh dear," said Kateřina, her face half-hidden in her headscarf, "I have a baby and I'm pregnant again, what am I going to do?"

"I," some old biddy replied, incensed by such weakness, "I raised three kids without a husband. The lad will grow, you just be a bit more careful what you do, for the time being you can work as well as any man."

They upbraided her as if at that moment upbraiding were uppermost in their mind, seizing on the most unseemly words, for no one is so simple as to put their fellow feeling in kindlier terms. In the end, they had to stop chattering and get to work. Not even war is a big enough thing to keep you from working. Terror and sorrow must not eclipse night and day.

Meanwhile, the district sheriff had hauled himself out of his basket chair and with the aid of his entire office concocted a kind of vacuous, yet still brazen exhortation to labour on, though at Ouhrov it was only actually read by the steward at the grange. He carried on with his rounds and was indefatigable in his urgings, repeating as frequently as he could ten words, of which the most frequent was *victory*. Rendering the war more commensurate to his own wits, he cobbled together ordinance after ordinance, direction after direction and

report after report; as of now, he was certainly short of both time and respite.

Ouhrov, habituated to holding the braying of officialdom in some small regard and being little inclined to heed it, ignored this discourse as was its wont. Farm labourers are indulgent.

From a compulsion resembling *Cholera nostras*, silk-stocking girls and some weedier males from nearby towns arrived at the Ouhrov estate, rolled up their sleeves and got down to work.

"I can be of use to you in two ways, with advice and with my labour," said the most dauntless among them.

"It'd be better," said Jakub, "if they'd cut out some of their mischief," but Ber took a different view.

"There's no harm in a bit of mischief and I'm sure these beer-cellar ne'er-do-wells get up to even more priceless tricks. Like putting out street lights, ringing midwives' doorbells, switching shop signs around and farting in church, so, why shouldn't they play the giddy-goat for our benefit now. What's so bad about letting the actions of this Foundation of Fun thrive and having a good laugh at them?"

"I don't know what there'll be to laugh at when they cripple the horses," said Jakub.

Anyway, one of them, who seemed particularly keen, adopted a wide stance, grabbed a pitchfork and started shifting some muck in quite a handy manner.

Finally, after two days, the helpers left with a sense of satisfaction, as if they'd just passed their school-leaving exams with distinction.

"Good bye," they said as they left, "we've worked as hard as we could, but our jobs in town (they were all, or so it seemed, clerical workers) are too important to allow us to stay longer. But we'll be back. We'll come again."

A few farmers, who were left beyond the bounds of the great estate, waved them off. "Our front rooms might be a bit cramped, but you'll always find a welcome. Come if you insist, your madcap goings-on are good for a laugh. You're hilarious!"

Sweat-soaked tenfold in their prunella boots, flat-footed and bow-legged, the helpers withdrew to their caves from the edge of a half-acre that remained un-scoured, like those warriors of legend who emerge to best the enemy in the hour of their people's direst need. Oh, this rampaging, this paroxysm of belligerence, perhaps matched only by the confounded stickling of railway and post office clerks, by now become so determined, this whole gory business that hadn't even been called a silly mistake! Pity the dullard who, if he'd taken less of a battering, might have had a go at any country outside the confederation of his Emperor! It took two years of battles and the unassailable certainty that the cause of Austria was lost for fellows to leave their Francis in the lurch and only save their own skins after their firstborn son had fallen and their youngest had been hanged.

Meanwhile work was pressing.

Whatever the war, whatever the plague, work has never subsided. Not an hour shall have passed without its being renewed at the end of days. It drives forward, turning the soil, sowing and reaping, and yet the call for bread is unremitting. An all-encompassing and most glorious campaign, a crusade whose knights have gone unsung, work, magnificent work, it is starting up again. Řeka and Jakub and all the workmen are at their posts.

Onwards and upwards! Let field mean frenzy, let it become bread!

Řeka, who might have been held to be mentally deficient by the court of patriarchs were he called to account for the crime of murder that he had committed, this man, who had grown old in his hallucinations and barely even registered machinery, mounted a motorised plough and managed to drive it up and down the Twelfth Mile until that vast field was well and truly ploughed. Indulgences under every legal provision might have been showered down on this head, which had not come to its senses even as the deed was done. Away from that terrible mental aberration, he was again without sin. The month of his madness had faded from sight. Hora's death was forgotten. Some new vicissitude, the like of which came in droves with every day that passed, had taken hold of him and in the midst of his labours he found himself musing on the strange troubles of wars. Small change, the only money of the poor, had disappeared and Řeka was having to reckon in whole crowns.

"What are we going to eat," he asked Jakub, "what are we going to eat of a Sunday if Lei won't give us change?"

"Come, come," Jakub replied, "when did you ever bother about money? How come you've learned to count now? Didn't you used to give Lei all your money and still be always in debt?"

Leaning against the cowshed wall, evening having bolstered his courage, he grew menacing and did not stop at mere advice. "Take a piece of string," he said, "and whenever you have a drink, make a knot at the end of it. Ten knots will be one florin, and if Lei cheats you again, I'll grab him by the beard and shake your money out of him. Don't you worry, František, and stop moaning."

"Yes," he replied, "I'll take an axe with me when I go, I've had enough of the fiend just like you."

However, the huckster's dominion was only just beginning. Sausages disappeared from his shelves and bacon slipped down into the cellar. "I'm cleaned out of food," he would say, "and I don't have a single bottle left. Aren't I standing here behind my counter, all set to sell, have I ever done anything else? These days, any heller I might make would be worth twice that to me. But sorry, I don't have so much as a half-ounce of dripping or a single shot of liquor."

The hunt for salt, run by a few smart individuals and a host of idiots, had brought him in a pretty penny, for this vulture was ultimately able to knock a few cents off the wheat they brought him. The clamour of numbers grew louder with every passing hour and every thousand soldiers, and Lei, who had readily ingested all the prudence of his profession, had heard the voices of war at the very outset. The tetchy, silly laugh with which he would round off his shopkeeperly pleasantries grew less silly and more tetchy. He could rail and sneer at poor women because fears born of war were his security and blood the rain that fell on his sprouting crop. He could rudely eject the beggar who, clutching his coppers, had dared to rear his head, for Lei had read the overriding view of the *Reichspost* on the results of the campaign. It looked as if the background noise of war had made it easier to articulate the ancient hostilities between workmen and merchants, between workmen and the farmer who employed them, between the baron's workmen and himself, between the workers and the voracious world that did no work itself and consumed all the fruits of their labours. It looked as if, within two years, this tinderbox would discharge sparks and a flame, though the labouring ranks are sapped not by fire, but by hope.

This was the start of a long time of misery, the crucifixion of the poor, the night and gloom of longsuffering.

The war dragged on. No one reared up in anger, and if some force did stir in defiance, it was pain. Poor village folk may have begun stealing, and they may have sold what they had received as payment in kind, all in order to afford to get drunk one Saturday or other, they may have been vile in their fornicating, but their grossness is surely blameless. All actions, all merrymaking and all sinning are masked by the gloom, murk and vapours of destitution. The court that will enumerate the culpabilities of sinners will not find Řeka's act of murder any more terrible than a lightning strike or a rock falling on a wayfarer.

After the first days of turmoil had passed and the Austrian top brass had descried the wide open spaces to the east, from the inner depths of the billeting office came an order, additional to the horses drafted in previously, for so many teams to be commandeered that they exceeded the total number of horses in the entire Empire by half as much again. Each team was to be accompanied by a man fully adept at working with horses.

The grange at Ouhrov could afford to ignore such orders, and yet the county sheriff, zealous to his own detriment, leaned on the baron as if he were a farmer.

Finally they did get a cart ready and select the horses. Then it came to picking a carter to drive them into the blazing inferno. Ber did a re-count of his years and Jakub did not want to go. So, the steward approached Řeka and said:

"You're still young and you've never been anywhere. What is there to it? Getting up on a wagon and driving off? You'll even get paid. Start getting ready, in three days' time you're to join the artillery regiment in Hradec."

"Me?" Řeka queried, "how can I serve in the military when I never went to school and don't understand a word of German?"

"It's all a lot easier than you think. You'll be following behind the rest and not have to do anything on your own account. No one will be able to tell you apart from the soldiery because you'll receive a cap and all the trappings of the army service corps except a weapon."

"Huh," said Řeka, "if they don't give me a sword and a carbine, I won't be a soldier!"

Before the day was out, the ox handler had swapped his shoes in the tavern for some high boots, paying two florins on top. At the time, wages had risen slightly because of the labour shortage at harvest time, and so Řeka had a few 10-heller pieces left over. Thus, like any new recruit, he could invest in a buttonhole and a round cap badge bearing the Emperor's initials.

"I don't have to pay you a single kreutzer and no one's going to arrest me," he told Lei. "No one's going to ask about your money, because it's all gone and all spent. In two days I'll be reporting in at the Hradec barracks."

"All right," Lei replied, "go choke on this crown, I can waive it for now since you're leaving; you can pay me another time. You surely don't want to cheat me out of my money, do you?"

Řeka almost believed himself to be the kind of man who knew what he wanted and could manage his affairs. He almost ate his fill and washed standing astride a pail, the way he'd spotted soldiers doing it somewhere.

The night before he left, some woman, whose husband had barely left for the battlefield, a woman who for years had surely never once thought of fornication, came to see the ox handler just because it was all too easy and all too likely to be forgotten.

His foolishness turned grave. He took her in his arms, uttering unfamiliar words, and the fornicatrix responded by shaking and teeth-chattering with fear. She needed the sin and the torment in order to find the tears that had already dried up. The door to the quarters of this farmhand, whose memory was like a sieve, had been open and nobody was watching it. So she had gone in, for of them all she was the most wretched.

In the morning, František Řeka pulled on his high boots and primped himself for war in the manner of all madmen. He stood awhile in the cowshed, talking to the womenfolk, while the men brought his horses out and hitched them to the cart.

"Good bye," he said, mindful of the night he'd had, "and see she stays faithful to me!"

"Who?"

"The old Vykusová woman," he replied, already up there on his box.

CHAPTER EIGHT

A vast force lay along the entire borderlands and he-wolves stared down from the heights and hills of the Carpathians. The Danube was studded with drowning soldiers, Belgium screamed its lamentations, and beside the Masurian lakes the death rattle of suffocating armies rose from the middle of the swamps. The fizz of pugnacity and the terrible vortex that uproots cities, the accursed power and valour of the unicorn, the forged steel wrecking bars, gullies and ditches filled with barbed wire, fire, aeroplanes that come sailing along and dealing death, toxins and gunfire, assaults by shades, assaults repeated ad nauseam and ad finitum! The mental degeneration of soldiers that can handle such horrors better than it can a spoken word. A brutish and obscene degeneration, blood that will return to a confused brain even from the cesspits and dunghills of battles.

Some twice one hundred thousand have fallen on the plains of this abomination and ten times one hundred thousand hasten on to the fields of war. Nikolai's regiments, Austrian armies, German armies, they shift from place to place and, bloodied by these horrors, press on towards their next encounter.

A fear-filled train rattles over the mountains and then across the lowlands and the cloud exhaled by the engine disperses over the keening landscape.

The hussars' red and blue has darkened, they are still laughing and can still chat about the trivia the day brings, and the regimental kitchen having gone astray, they wait for their lunch and their bread rations. They have yet to forget their tarts and any love that has affected them. They can still laugh after their own fashion, whether being borne along by trains or stuck in stations. Within this pack, snapped up from villages of every description, the officer still held sway.

Seven German armies, seven tornados of terror stretching from Aix-la-Chapelle to Mulhouse, set out on their incendiary and murderous way.

Who does not know the deeds of this bloodaxe, who does not know the deeds of these, the Kaiser's lackeys?

They became the clarion of devastation. Obsessed by a deception, they saw the seven swords in the skeletal right hand of von Schliessen. A cavalryman on a grey horse, raising his banner high, stood up in his stirrups and the men, numbering more than twenty times one hundred thousand, cried hurrah to the war.

Enter thou, enter! This is the land they call France!

Agreements are broken like a potter's wares and *right* is just a word.

Louvain burned and Brussels was taken.

Paris, Paris, here we come!

The terrible bow was drawn taut. Men had let their powers be taken captive and had become the stooges of governments, they had become drinkers of the blood that fuelled their rage, they had become angels of evil, devils who spilled blood like water. A raven with shreds of corpses still stuck to its claws was perched on their shoulder and yet they saw nothing and understood nothing. The orders of platoon commanders were their reasoning and a ghastly rough and tumble was their home, each such home perishing piecemeal as bayonets made mincemeat of arms rising to take aim. Death was made a day that had no sundown and horrors became the wont of armies.

The summer went by and terrible winter was drawing nigh. In the west, troops stood helmet-crest deep in graves and their bludgeoning abated.

Paris remained Paris.

It was fairly safe inside the city's whorehouses, in churches where services of thanksgiving were held, and on the Place de la Concorde, where captured banners were displayed. Paris carried on in its own sweet way, except that tailors, in imitation of death and soldiery, changed the cut and colour of their smocks. Nightclubs and dance halls filled up around eleven and at one ballroom the tragic seed of The Innocents was sown.

Those far-off times were cast under a somewhat slimy spell that had not been broken, for the agonies of the workers were not yet over and their grief lived on. The armies of France had put their faith in the heroism of battle and one tiny flash became a mighty flare, a fire in which the whole world burned.

Meanwhile, humble Russia – for the full measure of horrors and torments had not reached the peak required for it to rise from its bier – took to the field. Its four armies were like four villages full of merriment, superstition and a dread of killing. The traitorous von Rennenkampf was dashed from his desires by these peaceable fellows, who alone, apart from some Austrian corps, preserved a measure of reason. They proved able to achieve victory without madness, as befits an army, and to lose a field without the need to spray it with gunfire.

In the middle of August, the armies of Samsonov and von Rennenkampf crossed the frontier. The Cossacks of the Eastern Army marched into Prussia from the direction of Wirhallen, then the Southern Army immediately launched its own attack. Insterburg and Goldap surrendered to the Russians, for even old Prussia is just land.

Auf nach den Osten! Auf nach den Osten! A sergeant, tugging his drooping whiskers from regiment to regiment, repeated the Kaiser's call, and the various corps that had been readied to aid von Kluck's army turned eastwards. The horseman Hindenburg commenced his attack while the Russian armies in the middle of a foreign land had their heads propped up as they rested. The generals, perhaps traitorous, perhaps casual or just stupid, failed to make contact with one another and their flanks were not joined up.

Came the day that precedeth death.

Samsonov's army's patch, an area of deep marshes and shallow waters, scattered like droplets of mercury on a workshop floor, was encircled by a chain of the Kaiser's men.

In other times these men had sowed fields, worked on rivers and driven teams of three over great distances, but now all their mastery was vanishing and dispersing in jeopardy. They had walked over the marshland like walking on a lion, but now it was waking up, about to devour them. The forces pulling back from Allenstein ran up against forces fleeing from the south, and the horns of the crescent met. A blow was struck. These soldiers were like a flock who had been led to the accursed spot by trailing after their ram. They snapped their Cossack lances, once banner-decked, in two, gave their horses free rein and now waited in despair, for all their prowess and all their hopes had abandoned them.

The waters and the swamps rose up, overtaking the men's waists, finally to reach the armies' maws.

A gulp of air was going to be worth more than any Christian heaven.

Help!

Hear our call!

They were to descend into terrible depths with arms raised as in taking an oath.

Oh, would that the crude motives behind the slaughter of Tannenberg were better known, a slaughter that still brings the slaughterer a modicum of renown.

Would the maniacs arrive at a kind of kindred spirit, would they come to a kind of understanding?

There's no way of strangling a procuress as she hies away in pursuit of her métier, crossing the ocean by steamer, in steerage, so the papers would not have to suffer her snuffling for three days, but the man who had the guts to read all the horrors of this latterday deluge was beaten to a pulp in the street by the jackal-like lowlife of Berlin, and those who, having come to their senses, had left the quagmire after the Peace of Brest-Litovsk, were spat on by the rabble.

Disaster is one pinion of war. After the events in Masuria it could fly high into the sky, its terrible primaries casting their shadow as far as Kiao-Chau, as far as Tsingtao, as far as Africa. The most ferocious of spirits took up residence in the bleak lands of war and its dominion lasted a very long time.

Whole armies of reservists rushing headlong, again and again, to follow the flag, armies standing in the field before a chain of volley guns, jeopardised by them from the rear in no way differently and no less than by the enemy's, armies lured by the sound of drums amid apocalyptic horrors took aim at each other's hearts. Czar and emperors fanned the flames of hell in the east for the red of revolution to rise out of them over Russia and allow a star to be forged in this fiery furnace.

The Austrian generals Dankl, Auffenberg and Joseph Habsburg stood against the southern Russian armies advancing across Galicia. Boehm-Ermolli's troops had to be swiftly relocated to the Russian front for the Battle of Lvov, a battle no less fruitless than all of Austria's acts of war.

Outside Rawa Ruska, at the epicentre of this encounter, stood Ervín's regiment.

It was September 1st and evening was approaching. All around, in shelters set up at random in thickets and behind any slight elevation, lay troops not remotely resembling the hussars of Buda. The mettle exhibited so often in dance halls, the unabashed and persistent euphoria of combatants may have stayed with them for as long as they'd sat astride their horses. Those riders who had been charged with reconnaissance and forays had had barely a whiff of gunpowder, but at Rawa they dismounted. Leaving their animals in a poorly guarded enclosure, they took six hours to reach their appointed location.

"Halt!" shouted Ervín, leaning on the stick handed him by Jakub, "when will this damned jaunt be over?"

Both the far-off crump and the silence constantly broken by the hooting of owls had come to a standstill with them. Ears sharpened to catch every gust of the breeze registered nothing but the sounds of the forest.

"Walk on," he said after another expectant pause, distraught at his inability to cleave from crown to pelvis the nightmare surrounding them. They were in a forest quite unlike the grass-covered or bare-beaten ground of duelling pitches, unhorsed hussars in a field free of troops, in a forest free of all wild animals, without horses, without infantry, without kitchens, with a map to study and a colonel who had long since demonstrated his imbecility.

"Bloody forest," said Danowitz to the cavalry captain who was approaching them. "It seems to go on forever."

"So much the better," the captain replied, "because as things stand, death means nothing honourable where we're concerned. Say, Ervín, what would you give for a bottle of bubbly?"

The darkness deepened, the trunks of the trees grew closer and their branches drooped lower. The men went on, groping their way with rough sticks and carrying their rifles, resembling a flock of blind sheep. They went on, listening to the drone of war or to confused voices that were growing feverish. Ervín was resolute in his silence and his caution, no matter that up to this point they might still have brought torches and a drum to aid them on their way. The officer's dauntlessness turned silly in this time that went on and on, as if night were piling onto night to form a massif and a nightmarish gulf of ages. Going to war empty-handed or, worse, holding the crude weapon of the brawler, he crawled forward on his knees into some stupid tale, and certainly not towards a proper fight. He would fain have stood up in his stirrups, calling on his hussars, he would have gone ahead of them and, with his heavy sabre attached loosely to his wrist, he would have forged a way through the serried ranks of the enemy to capture their banner. But both forest and night were never-ending, five times they mistook their direction as they strung along behind the rump of the colonel's horse, which was being led by two hussars ahead of the troop, the colonel himself having fallen behind somewhere.

Morning was drawing nigh, night giving way to a windy day. The hussars came to a standstill.

"Danowitz," said the colonel, having regained his sway within the troop, "could you do me a favour?"

"For sure," he replied. "Shall I go forward?"

"Forsooth, you have an all too kind opinion of this day! There's no point in trudging on like this, the enemy is miles away. I can see nothing to cause us any disquiet, since from here we cannot even hear the sound of gunfire. Over there, sir," he said, pointing to some kind of gap, "is where the forest ends. That is our objective. So, will you press ahead so that we may be there before nine?"

Danowitz smiled.

"Before evening, Colonel, because a second night of this damned forest will be even more tedious."

Captains Vohryzek and Wess stepped up to the officers and greeted them as if night and morning needed to be told apart. "Good day! Good day!"

"Let's have breakfast," said the colonel, "gentlemen, have yourselves a cup of tea, as hot as a sacristan's candle."

"Hell," said Danowitz, "we might as well have stayed at home if this wild goose chase is what they're calling a war. The end of the forest, you say, Colonel? Far from it! This entire country is all forest, full of tree barriers all the way to the Russian frontier. I make so bold as to reject your view, sir, and suggest we go forward by day and by night until we get out of this snare."

"Snare? Snare? The word is too much! Have you gone mad following a bad dream?"

Danowitz responded with all the moroseness that he could muster.

"Leave it, Ervín," said Vohryzek, who'd been whistling one of those songs they used to sing that last summer in Buda. "Enjoy the forest for what it is, why dampen your spirits before it becomes unavoidable? For my own part, I find beauty in a dense forest, and among the host of other battlefields I can think of none that can compare with it for sheer appeal. Or would you rather be encamped before Verdun? Go take your big guns for a walk. Until lightning strikes and fire breaks out, let it just smoulder and fume."

Three days passed, another morn was breaking and it was almost five o'clock, and the forest, no less gloomy and bleak, was emerging out of the murk. A number of figures, more menacing than the shadows of wolves, were darting about its floor. The Russians were attacking.

"Who are you? Who are you?" Danowitz asked, raising up a soldier whose head was a mass of blood.

"Jakub," the dying man replied, raising his voice against the plaintive wail of gunfire. The vault of heaven of battlefields is generally a protracted, monotonous roar of ruination and any twinkling star, its wretched name barely uttered, is rarely seen to rise.

"I can't hear," said Danowitz, desperately placing his ear so as almost to touch the injured man's lips. The streaming blood and the word that had escaped them were not to return; Danowitz raised the nameless corpse. His wild imagination, which had earned its spurs, found expression not only in bravery, exhibited almost ostentatiously, but also in a crazy compassion: he felt duty bound to stand before each fallen hussar and raise over each corpse a cross with an image of Christ shedding His blood. The pinch of pathos which a kind of desultoriness had breathed into the Danowitz line, now, at a time when even the woodwork of wells was ablaze, flared up. In the depth of night he had pulled a glove onto his right hand to conceal some small, insignificant injury. It was again soaked in Hussar blood. He removed it and limned three crosses over the dead man while the others all fled in retreat.

The troop, which as late as the day before still had had time enough to experience boredom, keep trotting out jokes and be quite heedless of their officers, had been infiltrated by a pusillanimous, frantic compliance. Firing away, they advanced, dropped to the ground and rose again. Firing away! Forest fringes, sunken tracks, shallow depressions, all bristled with bayonets throughout their length and a myriad blue-grey fumes flew like leprosy towards the horrendous thunderheads of strife. Forests were ripped apart like linen cloth, falling flat and breaking apart like walls. A blazing inferno, anvils of hell and utter frenzy! Such frenzy as comes with every devastation and every pestilence! The fire and the dark, the tumult and the sudden silence drove whole armies crazy! The earth was splitting open and from heaven came conflagration.

"Where are we, where's the general and our colonel?"

Danowitz took the dead man's rifle and began firing. A soldier, seeking at least a shadow of calm, lay down next to him and three or four more joined this island standing out from the riverbed of downfall.

Noon drew nigh and the sun rose to its zenith. The last tear stood in the eyes of the dead and blood mingled with water flowed from their wounds. The battlefield lay wasted and the crackle and the tumult receded.

Danowitz was among the last to run. The nine soldiers he had acquired, who desired no more than to be saved aboard his craft and had taken the first lieutenant's bravery as their exemplar, ran after him. They had to stretch their cavalrymen's legs, for Ervín was now despairing, for it was getting late, for the battle was lost.

On September 9th the fate of Austria's armies was settled. The front was moving back and the terrible flight had begun. The brawls at watering holes, alongside cannon, next to ammunition trucks emptied of their load and driven by some good Schweik character surged towards the station, the fighting among the injured, perhaps more loathsome than the battlefield, the fire-raising, theft and debauchery of troops in defeat, repeated on all sides like the horrors of a flood, only made the war wider. Surrender to the spectre of war, pay homage to it, for war is hordes and you are a horde. You girt yourselves in a kind of bravery and placed your trust in the beating of drums. Be brave and beat that drum again. The clamour of battle has subsided and defeat rings throughout the land. Form lines on the San River or outside Cracow. Massacre the Jewish breed and the Ruthenians who have survived your cataclysm, violate the women. Wax terrible to requite your own paltriness. Wax more terrible than the name of pain, flame and glory.

The dogs of war went and hid in villages and several weeks passed without major incidents in the field. Russian armies were marching from the frontiers of Romania, along the ridges of the Carpathians, they stood before Cracow and stretched northwards as far as the borderlands of East Prussia.

Christmas was approaching and troop redeployments were reaching completion. Monstrous assemblies on the rivers Revka and Bzura readied themselves for the next encounter. That winter, the virgin forest of Skierniewice crystallised into snow stars. Two colours, dazzling white and dazzling blood, two colours and a night shot through with the fingers of searchlights, always on the move, two colours and a third night were the endless horrors of this section. Soldiers who had donned hoods against the cold of Russia could hardly hold their noisy rifles. It was freezing and the men shook in their tatters, dying to go back, dying to sleep. Naught could be seen but the dismal firmament, glimpsed here and there through the tracery of branches. Naught could be heard but the boom of explosions and the fizz of the frost. That thrust its way to the men's hearts. A hundred thousand soldiers froze, a hundred thousand soldiers were hit by this terrible weapon wielded by Russia.

The Germans reached these parts across open country, flat as a table-top. It befell to them to camp along the edges of forests that echoed to the sound of gunfire, it befell to them to haul heavy cannon to these locations and it befell to them to freeze, for fires are not to be lit alongside howitzers. The road to Warsaw led through this forest, Warsaw, of which someone said that it would decide the war. So for now the troops were poised.

Büllow's northern army, consisting of three corps, having carried out a quite extraordinary muster, proceeded in such a way as to outflank Mishchenko's force from both north and south. The troops advanced through snows, mud, waters half-frozen, thickets through which even a hunting dog could scarcely find a way, all to cries of the Kaiser's name. What sights greeted them over the land of Russia? They would have hurled themselves into a blood-filled pond, they would have slept in hamlets between mud and frost. At the Kaiser's command they would have flown high over the spires of Moscow and they would have nested in the forests like ravens. So, who would be so keen to get the better of a fury who can outdo them?

If the stories told are true, some Russian soldiers, considerably less eager to fight at Grajewo in the foul weather that descended on February 6th – when snow battled with rain, driving heads into every nook and cranny and covering every space in drifting snow –

than they had been outside Moscow in Napoleon's day, rounded up some pigs running wild about the village. The last of the porkers, having got stuck between a fence and the planking of a cow shed, was doing its damnedest to squeeze through the gap and abscond to the fields. 'Halt!' bawled a man according to the old army custom, a man who was reverting to his trade following its interruption by the call of the bugle. 'Halt!' He seized the squealing hog by a leg and dragged it into the middle of the yard. The animal was wrestled down to the ground and killed with a hammer blow to the back of its head, the way things are done at all farms whenever a hog roast is in the offing. They hung it up head down and the old butcher sliced it open less cleanly and more casually than was right and proper. It was gutted without scalding and to much laughter, because hog roasts are always fun. The wind buffeted the carcase this way and that, the flesh turning white and freezing.

Hell! In this vile weather a spot of hot dripping will be just the thing!

They were quartering the pig as the patrol three hundred paces beyond the village shouted the call to arms and Unburned Mill, as they call it hereabouts, was hit by the first shells. Nonetheless, they found their rifles and some cartridges and lined up, because the enemy was a thief and a killer.

The following day, in the north, the Russians began their withdrawal. They tried to make haste, but these armies of peasants only gave of their all, firing back from the ground cover by Pillkalen, once the cause was lost, as if each one of them were at risk of losing his very own fields.

While the remnants of Bolman's defeated army, to which the hussars of Buda belonged, were on hold, Danowitz caught up with his regiment. In these days of dread, when half the world was drowning in uncertainty, Danowitz was trying to find his horse. He was worn to a shred. Dispirited by all the proscriptions that so irk soldiers of the old school, of which he was one, he went from one equine field hospital to the next, past baggage trains and batteries whose numbers were being made up. He drank from every well, not giving a damn for the rubbish peddled by medics. He could open up a well as deftly as he once opened a bottle. He was a hussar among a rabble that more resembled market stallholders on a Holy Monday than soldiery. He put his ear to the very ground. Not a sound. He glanced over the troops. They were like an insect worming about inside a terrible, nasty sore. He might have raged like Achilles, but his tent stood open and no one summoned him. He slept, then, having come round, he stared into the candle flames burning on his table. He was dreaming and there was an echoing sound in his ears. A voice approaching a silent shore, a colour that had dropped into the motionless azure.

Sensing pain in the region of his navel and descending colon, Danowitz rose; he hoped to wait for dawn huddled up in his cape, for his bed had begun to feel strange. It was hot to the touch.

The fire of carbines and the dust he had inhaled are coming back. In times past, bright lights and music enlivened the early evening. One day, now long lost, he had been driving along the avenue of trees at Ouhrov and an old man, his head unprotected, was standing by his apiary. – The lights of the Somossy Orpheum gleamed no more.

Far away and undecorated, on the run and uninjured, Danowitz is to die of a vile disease, for it is easy to answer a question suppressed.

A painful and sordid death in the latrines.

Dysentery.

CHAPTER NINE

Fires in nine places in the east rose up into the cloudy heights. Paths veiled in darkness, fraught with perils, descended into Gehenna. For a hundredth time fires turned night into day, and again and again the starving pack lined up, clattering their hardware. Any glory had been stripped from these hordes forever and the name of soldiery taken from them. The breathing of bodies is held in aversion, and, should anyone look up at another, he, before uttering his imprecations, should stand in awe with one finger on his lips.

Regard the high peak of the stars and the depth of the abyss. The herd, hurled together into a huddle, roars, and the common folk are in tumult, for blazing lights fly high and armies and strife forge ahead.

In the gullies of night the current of time has turned back in its bed and it flows not down and it moves not. No one has any hope of their leaders, who went mad long ago. The unprotected borderlands are filled with enemy tents and more and more troops are forging westwards. The spread eagles of Austria have gone, and the pride of sergeant majors has been dashed. All have been turned to flight and are on the run, Jewish ghettos and landed estates are deserted. The thud of horse hooves, the screeching of railways and the terror that has taken to the road with head bowed, the madman's cape and hair flapping like a banner and smoke all trail behind the shadow of an army that was. The frenzy of hurry and scurry that gathers speed as the way grows longer and numbers rise, woeful twists and turns, confusion and distress raise their voice to a roar that grows in might and mounts into a veritable tempest.

Istęba, the estate where drunken revelry was once the order of the day whenever Baron Maxmilián came for the hunting season, was becoming deserted and its cellar was looking desolate. The manor house had shrunk to a lodgement tramped all over by soldiers, and despite the mass of people it was empty but for Josef's sitting room. The building, being a barracks, had ceased to be a manor house. The servants had fled and the stud farm enclosures, once filled with horses, lay almost in ruins.

Josef Danowitz turned a blind eye to the rifles and jackets hung about a hat stand wreathed in legend, he ignored the soldiers, nor did he respond when spoken to. His enfeebled spirit, his lacklustre spirit, long opposed to carousing, having been somewhat spurred in that direction by his pilgrimage to Jerusalem, which had ended some months previously at this very spot, offered resistance after his own manner. By saying nothing. He might have been said to be deaf and to have lost his tongue. He was made aware of some of the soldiers' rampaging, he knew about the havoc wrought on the stacks of unthreshed corn that they eventually left strewn everywhere, but he did nothing apart from declining to take up with the officers.

"Leave me, leave me alone," he told the estate manager, who was pained by such horrors. "I cannot prescribe torment for these iconoclasts, but I do wish it on them."

Several officers, who even in the field belonged to the real world, looked in on Danowitz to encourage him to board a carriage and leave.

"Thank you," he replied, facing the wall, "thank you, I'm staying. There'll be no military action around Istęba."

"Steadfastness," said a man from the 11th regiment, who had known Josef's father, "steadfastness in your case is to no purpose. You may have a secret to keep, so be it, take it with you or it will be snatched from you, if you're keeping a promise, break it! Hell, standing on ceremony profits nothing in this day and age! Your books will be reduced to nothing! Escape! Get a move on! Thank God you're neither too heavy nor too bulky. Come on, put on your sheepskin. Come along, sir, there's room in the britzka. Hurry up, or from sheer courtesy and my friendship for the Baron I'll kidnap you."

"I ought not to decline such a polite invitation," said Danowitz.

"What? You don't want to leave? Then you must be out of your mind," the major exclaimed, leaning out of the carriage as it made to set off. "Priest!" he growled, cursing forlornly, "An idiot cleric who's said to steal gold-plated stocks from his father's desk!"

The equipage disappeared beyond the park wall. It was going up to four. Josef crossed the yellowed snow as far as the yawning gateway. He stood watching, yet the sight of this wintry Golgotha still failed to fill him with redemptive dread. He had stayed.

Two horse handlers, who had come to Istęba to remove the horses to the Ouhrov estate and who now found the stables bare, also had to decide what to do. It was Ber and Jakub.

"Look here," said the former, "if everyone's in such a hurry, it's probably time for us too. To hell with your fatherly excesses! Josef's knocking about in Przemyśl somewhere. Let's get going while there's still time. Who knows how the Russians would treat us, who knows what vengeance Austrian soldiers would wreak on those who have sworn falsely!"

"Stupid!" said Jakub, "Who are you bound to by oath? Nobody's keeping you, just leave, grab a horse if you can find one, it'll be one of the baron's since around a hundred and twenty of his have gone missing."

"There are questions," said Ber, "that go unanswered. Let's not speak of either treachery or loyalty, because at the end we shall be on that side where our final moment will have cast us and wedged us in. Do you believe,

Jakub, that your will, for all it's more determined than mine, will be able to achieve any better outcome? Those you've just seen running away aren't running away from the Russians out of enmity, any more than they marched into this war out of enmity."

"All right," said Jakub, "but let's wait just one day."

They entered a half-empty shed, stepping over the remnants of the bundles of straw that had been lying on the ground. Dusk was falling. They ate some dinner and Jakub, whose patience was usually in short supply, went off. As the courtyard emptied and the soldiers were departing Ber slumbered. A mite of silence or at least a measure of calm descended on Istęba. A Jewish child and some old women who had stayed on perhaps from doltishness or had been left at the margins of battlefields perhaps as a punishment, poked about inside some crates that had been stolen two or three times already, inside crates and among shells that could well have ripped them to shreds, the filth and garbage spread by armies from one realm to the next. Ten weeks spent in a miserable village in Galicia, where all seemed lost, had almost made a drunken sot of the old retainer. He had plenty of reasons to hasten away from this dump, and plenty of reasons to linger on. He did drink, and he found a trollop to sleep with him.

One noisy night, as the windows rattled and the rumble of wagons spun out into one long sound, in a blizzard of insanity, on a hideous night when the drunken herdsman was abed in the hayloft, huddled inside a bottle of straw and chilled to the bone, some old ewe, reeking of the sheep pen, came to find him. He saw her clamber up through the hatch and come to an embarrassed halt, since she could not see in the darkness and no one called out to her. Ber started to exhale as noisily as he could, unsure whether he wanted her to come or to pass him by. Finally, he felt the touch of her claw. He was amenable. They tossed about on his pallet, as revolting as rats, as gruesome as an animal carcase. The depths of the obscenities in which they engaged were almost agonising.

"Go," said the strumpet, "fetch a bottle of brandy, you can buy some from the Jew, Lei, he's got a couple of casks hidden away."

"Lei?" Ber exclaimed, almost brought back to his senses by the word, "I know that name. Can it be that the Ouhrov grocer has relatives in Istęba?"

"All Jews," she said, "are related to one another, and there's not a name among them that isn't repeated all over the world. Go on, fetch some brandy, let's have a drink!"

Having returned, he pulled up the ladder and they dropped the hatch cover, as if it were necessary to segregate a sodomite and sow who were lying together from all other abominations.

This day it was her night again. Ber waited. It was going up to ten and she had not put in an appearance.

"What can the matter be? Can her daughters have hauled her off to their lodgings? Bother," he added after a pause, "how stupid of me to wait for this night, which was meant to be the last and which has now fallen flat."

He rose from his pallet and, grabbing a wisp that he meant to light as a signal to his harpy, he went out into the yard. The bustle, which for weeks now had shown no sign of abating in these parts, had swollen and was akin to panic. No one appeared bearing any message, no one cared about the affairs of leaders, no one broke their journey. It was no longer a case of delivering and receiving blows. Infantry, cavalry, human herds, drovers, artillery clanging as when iron strikes iron, a stream, accelerating to the point of skidding, stampeding and tumbling, headed across the manor down the imperial high road, which passed right through it.

To the railway! To the railway!

The din, fit totally to dispel any kind of composure, did nothing to shatter the horse handler's asininity. He kept looking for his tart. One uhlan, evidently elated to be returning to Cracow, hit him with a log that came to hand, and his body of troops, the kind that suddenly grows fractious and has ever been hostile to those who stand in its way, repeated the blow. They might almost have beaten this paramour to death. He tried to sit up, but before he could move he was snatched and dragged towards an odd tangle of bodies jerking about like an enraged herd.

Danowitz came out during this fracas and, being scruffy enough to be taken for an ordinary bumpkin, for all but riff-raff had already vacated this zone of retreat, found himself in the thick of it.

It seemed unlikely that anyone would escape this web of confusion and woe, it seemed that the pack would trample underfoot this circuit of dread and their own selves, and yet they were moving westwards, on foot. Then came the forced clearing of those districts of Galicia that were in danger. Horses and people, wagons and loads, human wrecks falling, being pulled and pushed, horses' hooves and the bare feet of the crazed, the deluge and the whirlwind sped on and ever on. Making tracks off the beaten track, across fields.

To the railway! To the railway!

This impassioned and lamentable cry, reminiscent of the cries that echo far and wide from instruments of torture, went undiminished.

Run for it! Hurry! In the east the earth heaved and the west was plunged in an abyss.

Cannon began to boom and armies slithered on hillside snows.

To the railways! To the railways!

Danowitz ran on between his two retainers. He tried to say something, but they were not listening. He tried to stop, but they shoved him forward like a bulging sack. The darkness condensed into a gaping chasm of lunacy. They passed the mouldering and smouldering mansion of Danowitz's neighbour. The booming voice of a stray cannon reached them from afar. The crowd thinned and Danowitz could pause for breath.

"Go tell the first soldier you run across who I am, bring a horse or cart for me to ride on."

Ber did as bidden and in no time returned with an infantryman.

"I'll take you to the captain, sir."

"Let's go," said Danowitz, "let's be quick!"

Ber and Jakub followed them.

Hereabouts the enraged boar of combat managed just odd little grunts, but the sound was terrifying enough for people to flee like madmen from it. The tide rushed westwards, streaming down from the heights and rolling across the plain. Itself akin to an army, it stole as it went and, starving, might even have gorged on the thatch of cottage roofs. Eventually, the poor wretches did reach the railway line and, collapsing breathless, they waited for a train to assail with their lamentations.

Couch grass and stalks of other grasses – the kind that get caught in the shoes of reapers – might suffice as an image for the poor folk who latched on to railway engines and trucks.

Sullen, grimacing corpses lay at the foot of railway embankments and new unfortunates fell down to join them. Well may one wonder what owls flit about these cemeteries.

Danowitz and the officer, who was genuinely undecided whether to believe the priest, who was almost chummy with his servants, reached the railway station the following day.

"My brother Ervín," the priest said, "is serving with the Buda hussars, I'm the son of Maxmilián Danowitz, he who is kindred with the family of General Sties."

"Pah!" his protector replied. "Can you also call on your fellows here to support your claim?"

"I could indeed call on them, they are our retainers and were born on my father's estate."

"All right, so be it," said the officer. "We'll have plenty of occasions to meet. One Danowitz of whom I have heard tell and who you do not resemble at all, was ostentatious in dress and general manner, and you claim he is your brother? Hm, it strikes me that you find worldly things distasteful, and even the things of your own station in life, since, for all you're a cleric, I did find you among a heap of men, two of whom seem attached to you in a most unretainerlike way."

"Sir," said Joseph, striking a pose like old Danowitz, who'd never taught his sons humility, "I confess that I should rather run for my life with the pack from which you plucked me than try to convince you on some cart that I am telling the truth. What should I have done with these two men? I set out with them, Colonel!"

"You were leading them and at just the right moment you saved them at my expense, for, as I recall, one crate had to be thrown off the cart so they could have a seat."

"Yes," Josef replied, "you could be right; we thought we were boarding an officer's conveyance, not a stage-coach."

"You shouldn't be so argumentative, except on questions of faith," said the colonel, opening his cigar case. "Let's have a smoke, sir, I believe you without reserve."

During this conversation, the ravaged landscape, tailing away behind them, struck Danowitz as no more than the backdrop to scenes of his mortification. He was a baron and his barony was unverifiable. The days of self-denial, the days of his pilgrimage to Jerusalem were gone.

They finally alighted and elbowed their way into the station, obstructed by crowds and the sorry freight of fugitives. They had to wait. Josef sat down on some sacks, but some men chased him off, cursing, and gave him a kick for his audacity. He felt faint and hungry and wanted to sleep.

Ber, who had been abandoned by all thought of his Istęba jade, was wandering about the station, looking for something to steal, when, passing a group of Jews, he spotted her prancing about in their midst like a chicken preening itself on a rubbish heap. He watched her, itching to give her a slap across the face, for breaches of faith are punishable in all circumstances.

"Come here," he shouted, pointing to his feet.

She rose and obeyed.

"You ate out of my hand, you drank my booze, yes or no? Well, I'd like my bacon back! I'm starving!"

"Ah," she said, "let me tell you why I fled ahead of you, I can tell you every detail about those last days at Istęba."

Ber followed her with a nod to Jakub. When they reached the planking of the platform, he hit the woman in the face. No one made a move and then the hussy opened her holder and took out some food.

"She's a bitch!" he said to Jakub, putting all his acquired wisdom into the word.

"You're a fool," said the cowhand, "if you've only found that out just now."

"Just now," he said, with a growing sense of shame, "she stole my money. My work pass. And a teacher's ABC book."

They shared a chunk of pork and left Danowitz the smallest portion.

After hours of almost lethal expectation they reached Cracow. Now it was up to Danowitz to make the requisite arrangements, for from here onwards fares had to be paid.

"War," said Jakub, "is a trap for numbskulls. If you were any use, we could have been inside Russia by now and me with my son."

"Why didn't we do that? Fear?"

"Maybe," Jakub concurred.

Danowitz spent the first night in Cracow sleeping crouched between his cowhands, resting his head by turns on one or the other's shoulder. It's possible he felt that he had been entrusted to them. In the morning, he stood up on his weary legs and after having his first wash in seven days, walked into the city.

Cracow was gutted, like a hive jogged by a careless beekeeper after the combs have been removed. Horseless cabs stood in the streets, holding their shafts high like open arms. People were living outside in the streets and houses stood empty, some of the townsfolk having left in search of a more secure refuge. Danowitz paused at a crossroads and, keeping ever to the roadway, changed direction. He had the illusion of some friend expecting him, somewhere nearby, and that all it needed was for him to call out his name and he would appear and guide him to his home. But it was midday, then three o'clock approached, and he was still alone.

"I have a feeling," he thought, "that the story with the colonel will repeat itself." At last he was standing at the door of the Commander of his order.

The clamour and clatter so long perceived now passed his senses by and the features of the high-ranking priest emerged out of a spectral haze only at moments. He sank into an armchair as if struck down.

"I'm here," he began in the locution of fevers, "in the place that I've been at great pains to reach. Give me some wine and make me up a bed. I am returning from an expedition which has not been a crusade. I am returning from a journey to Jerusalem. So, be lenient with me. I have with me two comrades who would be sad if I did not rejoin them and if they could not see me. Do find them. We have been terrified by a pillar of fire and a high cap of smoke and we are still in a state of fear. We set out on our way with no creature comforts, but now we are returning, having witnessed too much. The times have changed. Come night and there is no peace, come the day and there is no light."

Ber and Jakub waited in vain for Josef to return. He had wound up in hospital.

"It it weren't for the baron's lad and if I weren't waiting for my own Josef, we could climb on to the roof of a goods wagon. You can see that's how people travel," said Jakub.

"We've no other option," Ber replied. "You can't be thinking that our priest's coming back and that you'll find your son, can you?"

Two hungry days passed, spent on searching. Soldiers passing through Cracow could tell them nothing about the Buda hussars.

"We haven't seen them since the war began," they kept repeating. "They could still be lounging about in stables somewhere."

"Well," said Ber, "there's a train ready, let's board it, I've had my fill of stupid soldiers, and frost and Poland. Come on."

They climbed aboard, claiming their luggage was already inside. Jakub was just as good a liar as Ber and equally good at defending his position. Snow was falling and getting driven in through the cattle truck door.

"Ugh," someone gasped, mouth wide open, "board up that gap, it's cold in here."

At last the soldier in charge at the station brought the order from the good lord above, as the saying went, and the fugitives were able to leave. The train lurched a little way westwards and came to a halt; the line ahead was blocked. The waiting held the train in a rack-like grip. There was a stench of latrines, chlorinated lime, sulphur, smoke fumes, the insides of the trucks, bodies and the entire terrible load of fugitives. Eventually the crate-loads of adversity began to move, the points clinked out the moment of departure and a wedge of night wind made way, going against the direction of travel. Smoke like a widow's veil swirled in honour of all the dead.

They reached Ouhrov on the ninth day.

"We're here," said Ber as he removed his lice-ridden coat, "we're here and I'm damned surprised we made it. If ever there's any call to go to Istęba, do go, what we saw is worth a look. Jakub wanted to wait for the Russians to come and take us back with them, but I didn't want that. You can do it for me, their troops are already on the border with Moravia."

In those times, the strangest things went on in the simplest of ways. Discernment was stranded in time and the good people of Ouhrov could not care less about martial glory. That had demonstrated its folly itself.

Let the Russians come all the way to Ouhrov, let them come and dash the profiteers from office, let them wipe out the high prices! Let there be an end to the nonsense of ration books, let them come! If only soldiers might come home, if only the war might end!

Baron Danowitz, having heard of the cowhands' return, entered the estate manager's office and had them summoned to him.

"So," he said, tapping his riding crop against his high boots, "they tell me you've been to Istęba. What's new there?"

"Well, sir," Ber began, "of all the horses we only found twenty, but even they got stolen in the end."

"So I've heard," said Danowitz. "What else?"

"Baron Josef stayed at Istęba to the end, we only took him away when the line of retreat was being cleared by force."

"Yes, Josef *was* at Istęba, but *you* didn't take *him* away," said Danowitz, regretting he had spoken to these retainers. "You shall have your recompense," he said as he departed. Back in the house, Maxmilián summoned his Frenchwoman.

"Madame, I'd like to ask you a kind of favour," he said. "Josef is so absent-minded that he forgets who he is. Now, before he left, he took from my desk a paper of considerable value."

"I know," said the Frenchwoman, and Danowitz, suppressing his surprise, nodded to her.

"So much the better, I didn't say he stole it because I didn't wish to appear severe. Josef remained at Istęba until it was invaded and in the end he was hauled off to a station and put on a train. I've had a letter that says he's in Cracow, in the hospital of the Brothers of Mercy. I would be hugely grateful if you could go and visit him."

"I can't leave until tomorrow," she replied.

"Good. Take two footmen with you, since travelling these days is fraught with impediments."

The old baron dispensed with the kind of amatory display that he was wont to indulge in and with which he was unstinting in even less fitting circumstances. The hussy left with barely a good-bye.

"Well, well," Danowitz mused, once he was alone, "I've grown cantankerous and cannot tolerate infidelity, or loutish behaviour, the way I once could. If my mistress was at all involved in Josef's thievery, I shall send her packing just like him. I have dwelt in too diverse circumstances to have learned to be surprised, but as far as I know no previous one has been like this. Indeed, I did not believe myself old enough to be cuckolded so roundly."

Ouhrov's evening and night passed over Danowitz's wrath without softening it. He rose with an oath.

At that moment, a postal messenger, wide-eyed at the honour of being involved in the baron's proceedings, was banging like one possessed on the manor house door.

"What's the bother?" the porter asked as he took possession of a telegram.

"Baron Ervín may have died," he said, not making to leave, as if there were more he could say.

The news went all round the house before returning to the baron.

"Get a carriage ready, I shall be leaving before noon."

Injury exacerbated by insult and insult aggravated by injury did not leave him incapacitated. He glanced at the scoffing mirror, which endlessly reciprocated the old stance.

Danowitz, who was to stand bolt upright at a death bed, and a beggar, crawling up on all fours, a beggar's crutch, an escutcheon, a beggar's sack and, finally, two skulls. The two skulls crudely depicted on street corners, which crowds once tried to enchant into speaking.

All the baron's painful and humiliating memories coalesced into the hiatus of this journey. The rattling and rocking of the train reiterated them with such eloquence that he cursed his passionate temperament. What was needed was for old age to descend on this now almost white head to the sound of a thunderclap. It needed his vanity to be hit hard so that he might be a real old man; it needed the foolish delusion and action of a madman that he might turn in the dust. There's no telling if Ervín's death would suffice.

The copper sky, seen through the window, darkened, twilight began to close in and the landscape that described a circle around the observer moved backwards like the sections of fan opening out. The journey went on and on and now the frontier was not far away.

Meanwhile, all talk at the grange in Ouhrov, whose own pains are invariably in evidence and are, at the same time, invariably exposed to the ridicule of those having the courage to laugh out loud, was of Ervín, as if he were already dead.

"Old Danowitz's love," said Jakub, "was misplaced and he was deceiving himself in giving the older son precedence over the younger. Ervín is dead, but in defence of the other it has to be said he was a fighter. Josef was the better of the two."

"He was mad," they replied, "but how magnificently so! Your Josef's a ninny."

"A slob," said Ber, "can I ever forget the way he scoffed our meat then disappeared the minute he reached Cracow? Dammit! We waited three days for him, to bring us the money that he did owe us after all."

"In wartime," said one of the men, "all kinds of misfortunes come along; it isn't that bad to kill time in Cracow, or to be let down only a day's journey from home. And I don't think it's that bad if someone's in hospital, even if it's for dysentery. I know soldiers who'd gladly have swapped places with you and Danowitz. Maybe he was just malingering, like all those other malingerers in hospital."

This first winter of the war already found the grange without enough wood, or coal, to keep the boiler going. Five women cooked on a single stove and the men sat about on crates, or baskets, in the cowshed. Lei grew more lukewarm in his courtesies and the tavern remained closed all week. Customers had to knock on the Jew's window and wait until the usurer was ready to accept twice the price for his liquor. Ouhrov slept and grew torpid. Theft was on the increase and the fornicating was more shameless than at any other time. No secret was made of the horrendous intimacies taking place in the nooks of stables or in haylofts. War is a cloud that shrouds everything, an intoxication that lasts for years.

And yet! Sometimes you might have heard, at twilight, around the stove, for which a modicum of kindling had been found, the beginnings of subversive talk. This was the start of an apocalypse, which has by now been largely forgotten. Poets waxed lyrical over a legend with a beautiful ending, but above all a view was taking hold that did not mince words and was impartial in its judgement.

CHAPTER TEN

The open space, once known by the name of Spitalfield, wedged between the cemeteries and outermost projections of Hradec, the city's untilled rubbish repository, a scene of reviled bouts of love-making that almost counted on the grave for support, a site where all things nasty are in perfect harmony, was made the assembly point for those wagoners who were to set out after the army. They stood beside their horses, keeping military order as meticulously as possible.

Dusk fell, water needed to be fetched in pails and fodder fed to the horses, but there was no sign of the corporal, and none of the soldiers who had no involvement in such matters knew when he would be coming.

"How should we know what he's up to?" they replied, "he could have gone to the pub, boozing, or he could be smashing up brothels. Anyway, what's your hurry? In the army there's always plenty of time!"

"That's all well and good, but does the same rule apply to our meals, or to horses who have to be fed and watered at the right time?"

The young rustics lapsed into silence. A bird flew across Spitalfield and they watched it, keeping their thoughts to themselves.

On the stroke of seven a new horse and cart drove up under the watchful eye of a soldier, heading straight for those already lined up.

"Stupid! How are you going to turn round? Back up!" they shouted at the driver, who vouchsafed no reply.

"Bah," said the soldier who had been accompanying the wagon, "leave him, he's an idiot they've sent from some village or other. He was acting up like crazy so I had to come with him, I just can't wait to be shot of him."

So saying, he took the reins and, turning almost on the spot, drove off to the far northern corner of the area, least densely covered in wagons. Řeka followed his team.

Having dealt with the matter, the soldier mellowed and gave František several pieces of sound advice.

"Above all, don't go overtaking and don't freak the horses alongside you. Hell, do you know what that might cost you? You could get battered and lashed beyond recognition."

"Oh yeah!" said František, pointing to the ghastly scar running across his wry features, "I'm not new to such larks. Anybody who hits me could come badly unstuck."

"Pull the other one," said the soldier as he departed, "I'd say that scar's more down to an ox's horn than a knife."

Amid the rising ferment of the fighting spirit and lusty vainglory rising inside him, František might even have claimed to have stood with Radetzky at Solferino. Once alone, he swung his whip to describe a huge cross, then cracked it the way he used to each time he drove out through the gate at Ouhrov. Then he unhitched the horses, hung bags of oats from their heads as had been the practice on the more outlying fields and set about finding some water.

"Where's the well?"

"They bring water out to us in long wooden tanks," said the man standing closest to František.

"Aha," he replied, "so what shall I give my horses to drink if the water runs out?"

The wagoners' business was to stand by their horses' heads and not to move until the time came to depart. Řeka had been rather slow to acquire this art. He was constantly having to watch the others to appreciate all their strengths, and he was forever up and down by the wheels and traces, which kept slipping. He was a clown and all that is magnificent within the deeper recesses of even a madman's mind was obliterated in his actions, his leaping about and the stuttering that snagged his every movement and his every word.

"The man's mad," Řek's neighbour thought, "is he homesick or might he just run away?"

The carters stood in silence to the echo of the last words spoken, the suppressed storm and the background noise brought with them in their memories to this Spitalfield place. Their affliction was not well-founded, since these were no troopers, but war's mere stable hands, liable to be hit by no greater misfortune than the pittance they were paid. No one struggled to reach the station on their account, there was no waving them off, they could not mope without looking ridiculous.

They stood by their horses' holding points, alas, so rustically ramshackle, and mimicked the posture of soldiers, though if anyone yielded to weeping, the bumpkin in him was plain to see.

"My name," said the peasant wagoner who was watching František Řeka, "is Jiří Klika and I've come from Nová Ves."

"Where's that?"

"Not far," he replied, "if they'd let me turn my horses round, I'd be there in two hours."

"Aha," said Řeka, "stay where you are, I'll stick behind you and help you if anything happens to your horses or wagon. I've brought several rivets, nuts and a monkey wrench."

"You can keep your nuts and rivets! There are plenty of smiths around to look after the carts assigned to them."

"Honest, though," said František, "I'm good at it! Only the other day I tightened a bolthead that had almost parted company with one axle, did it as well as any blacksmith. I can do it again for the benefit of all the artisans on this site. I'm a dab hand, dammit, do you suppose I've learned no trade?"

In František's words there was none that he could have uttered at Ouhrov, and they conveyed naught but his fear of remaining a dullard.

Dusk was slowly turning into dark, the array of horses and the line of wagons were growing longer, seeming to stretch all the way to the skyline. The two soldiers attached to each team made bonfires, and the farmhands exchanged glances, wondering if this oddity would be permitted to them, too, since they were almost in the town. They collected some bits of timber or brushwood and made little piles that barely smouldered. They resorted to lying down by them, as they used to when out pasturing animals, and blowing into the embers to create a flame. Then came a slight breeze, more audible than gusting, though it did set the flames' tips aslant. Řeka, who was closest to their fire, was moved to rise.

"Hey," he said with a broad sweep of his hand towards the lights, whose number was approaching a hundred, "look, they've started fires and if it came to it they won't know how to put them out. Are you going to stamp them out, like they do in the village, or are you going to keep watch till they burn out?"

None of those sitting round the fire replied. Something impelled František to go the length of the line, from one huddle to the next, from one bright light to the next. Here and there someone voiced their animosity at the madman's qualms, and a shadowy red face, forehead, hand or menacing finger was raised at him.

"Hell, man, can't you see we're asleep? Mind you own business and stop bleating!"

Řeka had expected better responses; he was resentful. Finally, he crawled under his own wagon and, curled up in a ball, slept as soundly as at Ouhrov.

Five days passed. Řeka learned the rules of the encampment and now knew he had to stay in line and not address people who were not wagoners without good reason. Things were complicated. The men had to fetch soup in a pail slung on a crowbar, which flexed. Then you had to take your bowl and push your way through towards the cook. The server was not apt to concern himself with those who came late, he was impatient and his ladle banged against the side of the pail.

"Give me some soup, my fair share of meat and some bread!"

You have to shout and not scoff all your bread on the first day. He acquired a belt and girt himself tight, fastening it round his gourmand's belly in the most soldierly way he could, and yet he still was not entirely satisfied. The tatters to which manorial drudges have been condemned since time immemorial had stirred in him a liking for military attire: the belt, the weapons, and the gaudy plume that was beginning to disappear by then.

"Damn," he said to Jiří, investing all his chagrin in a single sigh, "where's the battledress, as they call it? Where's the brown and red of the transport corps? The soldiers look like grey rats and we look like the types that cart away wagonloads of sugar beet." The frippery and general aspect of the military, though no longer quite what it once was, struck him as supernatural.

"We joined the army too late!"

Meanwhile, in the affairs of the wagoners one order came hard on the heels of another and any later one was generally no less stupid than the previous one. No one knew what to do with the creaking wagons and all those animals and men who had been drafted in with such urgency. Ultimately, and surely for no good reason other than to be rid of such troublesome mouths to feed, they sent them to Kroměříž.

The teams of horses departed in some twenty sections early in the morning. It was cold and they proceeded in the customary manner of wagoners: sluggishly, drowsily and grudgingly, which left even Řeka at a loss. He looked scornfully at his empty wagon.

"Ah well," he said to the soldier who, finding his stupidity more rational than the taciturnity of the rest, had climbed up onto the box beside him, "yeah, it's all gone cockeyed. We thought we'd be transporting the general to and from his meetings. Unladen, with side planking or without, we've covered next to no distance at all, and we're all from estates where we have to flog our guts out. If only you could see what it's like to break in a stallion or drive with young horses that aren't properly used to the bit!"

"That's as may be," František's companion replied, "driving wagons is hard enough, but what's that compared to the job of an ox handler? What a grind that is! What a toil, keeping your team in check not from a box, but running alongside. You can even get your block knocked off! Then how about this: a short-tempered ox with a sensitive mouth can chomp the bit and go charging up hill and down dale for hours on end!"

František, happy at the chance to correct an assertion in which he saw not even the slightest hint of mockery, said:

"You wouldn't know where to start if they put you in charge of oxen! I've been handling them for many a long year and I could tell you a thing or two about how awkward they can be, how they're never in a hurry!"

The way progresses at an easy pace. In the evening, they would light fires and they spent the nights in fields of stubble. They rose with all the noise of an army and the racket from their encampment, unthreatening as it was, would lure an entire village, gawping, all the way out to see them. In some town or other they were given trench coats. So, were they any worse than those reservists kept behind the front lines or the trash in the kitchens who'd never lay hands on a bridle?

Having loaded his wagon with a dressing station, complete with its poles, canvas tenting and Red Cross flag, František was happy at last: he had been made a standard-bearer, placed in charge of the expedition's banner. A wagon so marked could not be overlooked, its driver's hideously striking get-up drew attention to itself and his name was beginning to mean something. He perched on his seat with his coat slung round his shoulders and sleeves empty, no matter that wintry days had begun and it was freezing. He spent the evenings chatting to the country folk, spinning yarns about his travels and the field of battle, as if he was just back from the war. His idiot's beardless face had brightened with the lustre of some feat. The days of axe and rope were behind him. Apart from his stammer, tales of events that had never happened and the odd fantasising, he seemed like all the other men. Remaining only at rare intervals a lunatic guilty of murder, he could reply joyously and adequately to all questions related to the service. He had become a soldier.

The sheer scale of the things to be done was his crutch, the host marching unhurriedly was his support, and he could keep pace with them. If it were not for all those damned cockades, stars and the tinctures of her-

aldry, if this expedition had been for work and if he had not loved soldiers before he became a man, František Řeka might almost have grown wise.

During the long drive, sensing the horse-shoe tread that will ever be ignited by bell, drum and clarion call, sensing this rhythm, he dreamed up his heroic homilies. So matching his words to the only book he had ever been read to from, he spoke as loud as the racket produced by his wagon.

These tales told finally became too sublime even for their mad narrator and František was left grieving for all that was unfulfilled and all that passed him by.

"See," he said to himself, taking out the document that he had stolen from Baron Maxmilián's desk, "see, I took this paper, half covered in writing, half clean. If I'd wanted, I could have taken the money and everything else. I can have, if I feel like it, money to burn."

One day, as Řeka was staring at his paper once again, the corporal escorting the expedition, aware of František's proverbial stupidity, wanted to know what he was so preoccupied with.

"What's that then?"

"Nothing," he countered, "just a piece of paper with an eagle that appears and disappears again."

"Well, well, where did you get that? It looks like a government bond or an old lottery ticket. Are you that rich?"

"I'm not rich," he replied, "but this paper with the eagle is left over from better days."

Several people craned over the corporal's shoulder to see the document.

"This?" Jiří spoke up in his turn, "I reckon it's no more than a French certificate."

"No, no," said the corporal, "it's an annuity which, if it were still valid, would mean twenty thousand crowns a year. Blimey, that'd be a tidy sum, Řeka!"

Then he folded the paper and returned it to František. Nobody doubted that it was no longer valid.

Four months later, the military command decided to use the Hradec teams behind the eastern front. They were to work on the construction of reserve fortifications just beyond the outskirts of Cracow.

František's banner and dressing station departed his wagon. He was given a mattock and spade. He was to work as he had been wont at Ouhrov.

"This war," he told Jiří, spitting on his hands, "is being waged more with pickaxe and shovels than weaponry. I've seen regiments with barely enough rifles, but hauling shovels around like day labourers."

A succession of days passed uneventfully and without glory. The troops' outward appearance, if seen at all, was deteriorating day by day. Patched trousers and coats stiff with muck, not at all matching, could have no appeal even for Řeka; nonetheless he procured such togs piecemeal until he was clad from head to toe like a soldier.

"You're a fool and a fool you'll remain, can you really be bothered by what you wear, can anyone be bothered, for God's sake, in this place, about anything more than eating, sleeping in the dry and finally getting away unscathed?"

"Armies have always been dressed in a particular way," Řeka replied, "if it's any different in this war, then things are far worse than they seem. By what sign are we supposed to recognise one another? Certainly not by language, for aren't they all spoken here?"

"Why should we recognise one another? I don't like being a camp follower, but if they wanted to treat me as a soldier, then I'd take to my heels and do a runner one day."

"Would you run off home?"

"No, to the enemy," Klika replied. "I wouldn't be the first: there are said to be fifty thousand Czech soldiers captive in Russia."

Some bearded almost fifty-year-old approached the speaker and said:

"What's so odd about that? It makes me shudder to think how many dads haven't ducked out yet. Well, are they supposed to hang on for the stinking cash paid out for bravery? I mean, death roams among soldiers like it roams about its own house, and no one's entitled to save his skin by fleeing? We can choose our own war, we might well end up shooting from the other side, but I don't mean to bite the dust in this benighted abomination."

František Řeka who, in the manner of all fools, would concur with the opinions of others even when it did not suit him, nodded. The anger and the cursing that he had been hearing daily for some time now, that and the terrible oaths and jeering scared him. He was too stupid a man not to love all things wonderful, all that shone in every colour, anything that resounded and reverberated. How could he know the truth? He was a murderer and was ceasing to be one, for incendiaries and blood-coated butchers had succeeded in making murder glorious. War had brought it out of the cowshed. He had been made a man by it. No matter how hellish the horrors of war, František could inflate them even more without any sense of disgust or fear. He would have waged war to the point of annihilating every living thing.

Hard by the fortification site where Řeka was working was the Brodce aristocrat-owned cotton mill; by this time it had been abandoned. The drive belts and machine parts that could be dismantled were packed by soldiers into crates and carted off, not far, to be sure, and in such a way, to be sure, that they could reduce them to smithereens en route. However, the boiler was left standing at the centre of the mill, a gigantic iron dome, a fearsome potbelly, rigged well enough to defy the vagaries of the elements or the breeze buffeting the door by the entrance to the engine room.

"This boiler," said the section commander, all of a dither, "could get stolen or broken. We could be in trouble before I knew it, but mercifully the danger has been recognised in good time."

So saying, the major opted for a true military solution.

"I'll have eight volunteers from the work company to stand guard outside the works!"

František Řeka had heard rants against physical labour in the army too often not to want to get away from it. Guard duty, that means having a rest and is almost actual warfare. He abandoned his mattock with the same ease as he had once abandoned his horse and cart. He was almost an infantryman: they had entrusted him with a rifle and bayonet. In the morning, as he was leaving his cruddy quarters, he cursed the major in the manner of all soldiers for plaguing him with that duty.

"Never mind," he said, "they'd rather make every man a soldier and be happiest shunting us all off to the battle line!"

Poorness of spirit made him adopt language as spoken even if it was not the way he spoke himself.

Having reached his new post with the others, he acquainted himself with all the corners of the building, much like a dog. He finally plucked up the courage even to go inside. A crane stripped of all its pulleys and chains, a broken-ribbed skeleton, gave him the same scare as a dangling corpse.

The memory of the murdered Hora entered his head.

"Where are you?" he said, "In your Smrdov grave! That's my secret and I won't tell a soul!"

Now every encounter with machinery struck him as hostile. He came back out of the mill as fast as he could, sensing something staring hair-raisingly at the back of his head. At twilight he made a fire as if meaning to do dinner on his own account, then once he was sure he was alone, he took out the paper from earlier in the day to incinerate it. It burned away with no semblance of an inferno. The wind took it. It disappeared and was no more. Řeka scattered the ashes.

"Hey there," he shouted at a man wandering about a few yards from the factory building. "Hey, Muttonhead, come here, I'll show you how money burns!"

Řeka had to be on patrol at six. He picked up his rifle and, pacing like a Prussian guardsman and tramping with his hobnails, he dreamed his turbulent and savage dreams.

"I'll grab a bottle in the inn at Ouhrov and smash it to pieces on the bar. Lei's got a belt with brass studs, so, I'll take a bit of broken glass, slip it under his belt and pull it tight, all the way to the last hole. Hold it, you dummy, you dragon, you minnow, bobbing there over your counter! You've been doing your mucky business here for quite long enough and for quite long enough you've been wearing that grin. I'll pay as it behoves soldiers to pay. I'll ask you about your relations and before I do a cock-crow you'll make me your confession."

The night murmured and the waves of darkness turned. The madman had been crowned king with a bayonet.

After a time, the prudent major was replaced by a less cautious sergeant. The Russian armies had begun to withdraw and the Kaiser's men were following them step by step. Again there was a need for two-horse teams and the general bethought himself of the wagoners from Hradec. Cracow was secure, so the army's horse handlers were dispatched twenty leagues to the east.

Řeka was assigned to guard duty, which he had already begun. He found himself among soldiers, and with the command of the unit to which he belonged changing a hundred times over, he finished up in a company which, though not a fighting unit in name, nevertheless made its way onto the battlefield.

By now spring was in the air and troops were gathered near Gorlice. The spirit of the German army, which dashed up to the clangour of its cannon, also came thundering along the iron road. An appalling battle was commencing. In the frenzy and the rampaging of the great unwashed all living things were trampled under-foot.

From the Dunajec river to the Dukla Pass cannon boomed, the air was filled with soil, fire, whizzing and thundering. For twenty-one days the battle raged and the now woeful armies carried out their orders.

From out of the chilling tracts of time not even this moment could rise up. Night passed and a May day bent its steps towards nine of the clock. Like smoke, the uproar of armies fanned far and wide, and the brume of imprecation, riven by fire, again and again became flesh. The lamentation, railing and the rattle of death begat the hideous and most human utterances of armies.

Two small hills, once trodden by bright-eyed bovines with bended neck, were split apart, life lay in ashes and the battered forest bristled like the spokes of a broken wheel with the felloes gone. In these horrors there is no greatness save the greatness of the destitution wrought.

Oh, thou might of armèd hosts, oh, ye words of mercy uttered and tears so manifest, ye are not, not, mightier than the madman von Mackensen astride his white horse! Despair ye, for military leaders do gamble over Gorlice and again over the San River and all places on the surface of the Earth. Despair ye, armies in retreat and armies victorious, for the general has not been taken and shall not be put on trial.

Rage hath sunk into darkness and the fire-spouting cannon now falleth silent. So, seek ye savage words, the names of attack, hatchet and the sorriest of slaughter. Neither dead nor living shall be heard, therefore be the column of silence uninscribed, be thou void! The ignominy of the inanity, obtuseness, submissiveness, dread, disequilibrium and inertia of hosts is plain to see.

This day of the battle in the lands of fertile Mościska, where the smoke-laden wind bore soil skywards and half-light rained down blows and fire, was paling now and fading away. A vast nothingness and air of futility overlay the battlefield; after a moment of such savagery time was needed, raise the floodgates! Open wide the doors! All the forests and all the waters are not deeper than time, for time is the roof of the cosmos, it is a shelter, it is repose and hope.

Go thee, make thy way through the pullulation of pain and the obscenities of glory!

A chink in the bright sky above parted the darkness and its glint fell in a silent, mournful ray on the most wretched and, in the parlance of soldiers, the least glorious point on this stretch of the battlefront.

The descendant glow, that tiny mirror of the sky and a shallow pool of hope overlay the blood that had already sunk in, as a right hand sets itself on the left when you clasp your hands. At this intersection of bright and dark, heaven and hell, lay the shattered body of Řeka. The ploughman of Ouhrov was breathing his last. Yet death was in no hurry, time kept standing still and coming back.

The simpleton, who, for three and thirty years, had been taken by bloated overseers, farmhands and serving wenches for a madman, now had no name, having tossed aside somewhere the card inside its metal holder. His name lay forgotten in the firmament of the poor and František would not now utter it, for his horrendous injury had torn out his tongue. He no longer stammered, but was wordless, he was no longer a man, but a mystery, the face of which was a wound.

They will gather him up and carry him back through the reserves and the triple rearguard, and this progress will remain forever engraved on the minds of those who witnessed it.

Slowly the vastnesses of heaven consumed the fury of war; the injured man began to regain consciousness.

Now, all about him, having outrun the horrors and the pain, was a muddy yard. See there, a chewed whip handle, messed up by a knife, snorting horses, an overturned harrow, and a barefoot maid carrying a jug and saying: I'm taking breakfast over to the field at Zastrov.

CHAPTER ELEVEN

The St Lazarus Hospital, an archipelago of despair in a north-eastern corner of Cracow, a ferry stage, a port on the Acheron, during this war the bleak hospital of Saint Lazarus had turned white. After the ferocity of battle, the clamour of the operating theatre, soon stilled, seemed but a sigh.

How foolish is impatience, this pain means six months out of harm's way. Well, aren't you glad you picked up such a benign injury?

Day after day they would haul a corpse from this prism of ease and load it onto a cart. A few soldiers would follow the corpse to the corner where the road bent towards the cemetery. This was the first stop of the cortège. The band finished playing and the soldiers quickly went their several ways, for funerals were held all too often and the days were short. The company would have saluted the deceased one last time with a carbine volley. Farewell, soldier! It's all over, hurry along, hop about inside your coffin. It's up to the living to measure time by their labours and to hasten towards their cessation.

A broad belt of greenery separated the block for conditions requiring surgery from the unit where Ervín Danowitz lay.

Morning was drawing nigh. The room which Ervín shared with two equally ailing officers stank to high heaven, foul beyond all imagining. These three or four wooden shacks were dreadful, yet they were furnished and fitted with everything that was wanting in the other enclosures for infectious diseases. Patients with dysentery, who certainly had no place in an urban environment or in the proximity of the wounded, only rarely came to the oasis of St Lazarus. For such a patient to be taken in he needed a barony, and at least the rank of colonel. The hospital's good name was not to be lost over one vile and stinking corner.

Ervín woke on the stroke of six. He tried to rise or, rather, crawl, sensing the cursed call of his indisposition, but loath to summon the sisters. He was almost alone, for the other patients still slept. Oh, how little he now resembled a single moment of his days as a hussar! He was a broken man, brought to naught. He had been rendered humble and small in the embrace of his sickness. His blood, once intemperate and fervid in the service of arms, weltered thick and putrefying in his heart, which could barely keep its stream boosted. Only his eyes kept alive the gleam in his features, a gleam of fever that was finally taking over from all his zest. Death stood at the head of his bed as a wagoner stands by the heads of his team.

That morning, the old baron finally made it to Cracow and, after a quick wash and brush-up at the first hotel he had run across and leaving his baggage, contrary to custom, in the care of a chambermaid, he made haste towards the gate of St Lazarus'.

"I can't admit you, sir," said the soldier whose duty it had become to act as gatekeeper.

"I know," Danowitz replied, "but I shall enter against your will. You can tell your commanding officer that I forced my way in."

Registering that the soldier-porter was set on having his say, Danowitz thrust him aside as if he were preventing him from entering Ouhrov.

"I'm Maxmilián Danowitz," he said to the sister dozing in the patients' anteroom. "I've come to see my son. Go in and ask him how he is."

In the little room, which spoke quite eloquently of the trials of infirmity, Danowitz's nerve began to fail him, though not because of any danger, which he had no fear of confronting and which he held in utter disregard.

"The baron is sleeping," the sister said, "but I am obliged to remind you of the doctors' strict injunction. These rooms are not to be entered."

"There you go again," said Danowitz, "do you suppose I shall turn back from this door?"

"Ervín, Ervín," he said bursting in, "have I come soon enough to take you away from this place? Couldn't they have found you a better hospital in Cracow?"

He gazed upon his son as if he were still a ten-year-old.

"Ah, you've come, father," said Ervín, offering him a hand, which fell limply into Maxmilián's hands.

The feverish air, full of the stench of dysenteric faeces, stirred and swayed with this headlong intrusion, like a cloud hit by a gust from the west. Both patients woke and Danowitz was impelled to apologise.

"It's been too long since I saw Ervín and a bit of commotion was inevitable. In my day, reunions were always noisy."

"I'm well enough now," said one of the two officers, "to move to another wing and leave you undisturbed. I know Ervín well enough, and you too, Baron, to foresee that your visit will do the patient more good than all the prescripts of doctors. So stay as long as you wish, it'll do me no harm or inconvenience because in the next room they're already playing cards and not far short of starting to smoke even."

"Your hospital isn't as awful as it seems," said Danowitz.

"I can't go," said the other sick man, his speech interrupted by silent pauses, "but do move my bed. There'll be plenty of opportunities for Ervín to return the service; possibly today or tomorrow my father will also come. And I'd also like to speak to him alone, because I feel I'm going to die. Ah," he sighed, rejecting all words of comfort.

Danowitz hesitated and a silence reminiscent of a ram ready to charge passed round the room. A silence such as Danowitz had never heard, a silence so unlike his books at Ouhrov.

"It's what I want," the soldier added, "it is, and I'd be embarrassed to ask the captain to leave."

So they bore the iron bedstead outside as if in imitation of a funeral rite.

"Poland," said the old baron, settling down next to the patient, "is a lousy country; if you'd marched west or south, you'd be well, or, even better, you'd be wounded in a manner that befits a captain, because, my lad, you *are* a captain! Your general has written to me on the matter of some decoration."

"Pah!" said Ervín, making a poor show of hiding his fatigue, "doesn't that sound like a travesty? Being appointed now, in sickness?"

"But that's almost over, it's almost the end of the tedium; now what's needed is for you to come back to Ouhrov and not go dashing off to the regiment."

"Regiment?" Ervín queried. "Do you suppose the Buda hussars are still a regiment? We've been wiped out. Half of us fell and we fled just as fast as we could. I've seen a man die and his name only came back to me last night. It was Jakub, son of the Jakub who works at the grange in Ouhrov. He tried to say something, some message that remained unspoken."

Death, hanging there over Ervín, lent his words a hidden significance.

"What became of that Jakub? May he sleep in peace if he's dead!"

The last, or perhaps some similar sentence would have been uttered by Danowitz with the greatest intensity, but he held it back. The gravedigger's shovel, already ringing out, was too loud, and the pile of soil, the wall of silence that would bury this soldier, doused his words as a candle. Danowitz could but grasp a frantic hope from the very extremity of madness, for this man was not wont to take things lying down and wait for disaster to strike.

"Heck," he said, "I'm dithering here as if I'd got nothing better to do. Where's your doctor? I'll go to him and ask him in detail about ferrying you out of here; I should have rushed off an hour back, because from now on every moment you stay here is down to my sloth. We'll have plenty of time to talk in Ouhrov, but now it's time to leave."

The doctor, who Danowitz did seek out, was stupid enough to think himself indispensable.

"No," he said. "I cannot allow him to leave," and when Danowitz persisted, he said: "You'll finish him off within two days."

Meanwhile, the Frenchwoman had sought out Josef; he was well and ran forward to greet her.

"They've been keeping me here for no good reason," he said, "but I think my detention's nearly over."

"Yes," she said, "you can go back to Vienna, the baron wants you to be treated by a doctor he's looked out for you."

"Thanks. I'll be going back to Ouhrov, I've never felt fitter than I do right now. I need neither medicines, nor medics, when's this misapprehension going to stop?"

Maxmilián remembered his second son only from necessity. The hospital of the Brothers of Mercy was far away, and the baron took a cab. The noise that he'd been accustomed to hearing for forty years had died away. His driver took his time and Maxmilián had had to sit through all the doctor had to say, which he repeated word for word. "Can't it be avoided? Is he really going to die?" he'd said, horrified for the first time. The St Lazarus Hospital had reminded him of a tomb and this trip, which only meant putting off speaking to Ervín, this trip to see his second son, which he wouldn't have been making if he knew some other way to postpone it, seemed to him to be unavoidable.

It was going up to ten o'clock as he climbed the stairs at the Brothers of Mercy.

"Look," exclaimed the Frenchwoman, having spotted him, for she and Josef were standing on the top landing of a staircase with two half-landings below. "Look, it's the baron, I recognise him."

Having climbed the middle flight, Danowitz found himself face to face with them and with each step he took he saw Josef rising from the ground like a rebuke.

"Good morning, good morning, ma'am," he said as he approached, "Did you have a pleasant journey? Sorry, I couldn't set off after you at once, because I received some bad news. Ervín has been taken ill. Both my sons are at death's door. Yes," he repeated without listening to any response, "both sons at death's door!"

"Take that coat off," he told Josef, who was still attired like a Hradec pauper, "get yourself ready, I'll announce your departure to the office and wait for you there."

"I've begged many favours of you," he told the Frenchwoman, taking her aside. "But it's all over now. We're well beyond half-way through our story. You have been most amiable, but I'm growing into a grumpy old man. All things must end, so, let's say our goodbyes! Oh dear," he said, noting that the Frenchwoman wished to raise an objection, "let's say our goodbyes with gritted teeth, the way things were done in my younger days, let me feel young this one last time. Go to Vienna, ma'am, for Vienna is most beautiful, and take up residence in my house on Ballplatz, you can have it. The lawyer I'll send to see you will take care of everything. So, that's it. Let's say good bye."

Danowitz doffed his hat and, only half-hinting at the usual civilities, opened the door of his carriage.

"Farewell!" he said finally and bowed his head to the girl for the last time.

Having gone back to the hospital office, he soon completed his business there, for both clerk and doctor trembled before the aristocrat.

"This baron," said the superior after Maxmilián Danowitz had left, "is the father of a poor soul who, each time he says his name, will be thought a braggart and a cheat."

One friar ran solicitously out to the cab stand and set about choosing one for the baron with the greatest care, opting for a team of large mares, black as night.

"Get in," said Maxmilán to Josef, who was coming down the steps. "Get in, Josef."

The horses trotted off.

"It's time," said the old baron, "to go over a number of matters. Before you set out on your journey, you took from my desk an annuity worth twenty thousand crowns. Did you sell the document? Come on, out with it! Did you sell it?"

Josef, who was paler than a sheet of linen, stood up, banging his head on the cab ceiling.

"Could I have been wrong," said Danowitz, "in assuming you'd be willing to speak of these matters that have already passed? Are you not ashamed to put on such a laboured pretence?"

"I never gave a damn for your money!" Josef blurted, having finally found his tongue. "You can swallow the lot! You can stuff your gut with Ouhrov and all your other properties, which are probably burning already anyway! Why do you have to start inventing such devilry when the day of reckoning is so close? You have squandered your annuities and assets, which weren't even fully yours, given you have sons to whom it appears you feel no liability."

"Enough!" cried Danowitz fit to frighten the cabman, who thought he had a lunatic on board, "enough, son! That's enough of such wickedness, rest assured that I'm sick and tired of it. I want to keep my composure," he added after a pause, "I'm old and your brother's dying."

"You're not old enough as long as your Frenchwoman's around, and I'm sure Ervín, if he is in Cracow, is not dying. That's not to say the tragedy of it doesn't suit your purpose."

"Stop, stop the cab!" Danowitz shouted to the driver, and before it came to a halt he had opened the cab door.

"Go and find the St Lazarus Hospital," was the last thing he said to his son.

Meanwhile, Ervín, stretched out in his bed, was fading fast. The other patients, except the one who was at death's door, had left, wrapped in heavy blankets, and had sought refuge in other buildings. Ervín Danowitz was alone, and the other dying man was alone.

The maidservants who had come in search of news were told by the nun: "We are expecting two dead men, they seem near the end. We expect them this evening."

The whore Tereza, who way back in Buda had had five names, had added a last name to the series. She had become a nurse. She was at the St Lazarus Hospital and kept asking after Ervín. The maids were her messenger girls.

"It's the end," they told her, "Ervín's going to die." She emitted a cry as terrible as the excruciating loves of whores.

Baron Danowitz is going to die! She took hold of a coat of sorts, which she drew over her head so that no one would recognise her, since she used to be a prostitute, then she ran across the frozen garden area and stood by the gate in the fence that separated the dysentery section. Perhaps she was hoping that death would step back once it saw a prostitute tearing at her face and weeping for her beloved.

Danowitz was dying. His pulse was slowing and his half-closed eyes turned up to the dark and silent mountain that looms above those at the point of death. It was going up to three o'clock.

"How is it?" asked Maxmilián as he entered the anteroom, but the nun left the question without reply. He entered and, pausing in the middle of the room, he tore off his coat. He could but grovel on his knees, he could but wail, he could but form sobs filled with tenderness such as he had never given vent to before and which he had torn from the very heavens.

Here he was, here lay his son, dueller, spectacular swordsman and debauchee. He who had taken up arms, Ervín Danowitz.

The first shades of night were descending and the day was over. Five o'clock struck and the prostitute was still standing by the gate. Catching Danowitz's name, she stepped back before a man who was making to enter. "He's dying," she said, "dying, and his father's with him."

The priest Josef, a chronic oaf, a devastated, slighted priest who'd done wrong and bore the hallmarks of madness, an outcast falsely accused of theft, an outcast half of whose sins were pure invention, had dragged himself this far both to his father and to his brother's bedside. Unable to find words of his own, he mumbled some prayers, newly recollected.

Some command given to the company lining up beyond the fence, audible even within, was the final reminder of the joyful, sprightly day when Ervín, standing at the head of his squadron, had slashed away at heads in the wind and, like a sower wishing to sow a cloud, brandished his hussar's sabre. Farewell, Ervín, all things come to an end. We have reached the end of our story.

Around nine o'clock Ervín died without a word and without any gesture that could have been a sign. They bore him off to the morgue through the blustery January night.

The baron and Josef departed. They walked in silence, unable to say one word to each other. They walked on, dragging their aged and feeble feet, for one of them was senile, the other indigent. The cathedral tower rose out of the city in its folly and impertinence, as if the heights of heaven to which its needle-like tip was pointing were not vacuous and as if something still endured in these parts. In the fly gallery of the night, stars shimmered, too dreadful to be any consolation, and the floor of the city teemed with gormandisers crawling to their taverns.

"What will you do, where will you go?" Maxmilián asked, breaking the silence at last.

"Where should I go but with you! I shall beg you not to think those wicked things, I'll follow you and keep repeating my entreaties over and over again. Now that Ervín's dead, Father, you are the sole Danowitz, since your second son is nothing more than an unworthy priest. Distribute your worldly goods to the poor, taking no account of me."

The feeble breath of death had given them all a fright and the prostitute had already left. Ervín lay alone in the St Lazarus morgue.

They shall dream of this hussar, who will once more go to war in his magnificent accoutrements. Again shall he mount his steed and call to account such windbags as dare to utter something opprobrious. Danowitz will advance in dreams and memories, pale and paler by the day. In the end he shall be as forgotten as he is now abandoned. Battlefield hotheads may crow, the mirrors in the Somossy may smash with a bang one by one. Danowitz has alighted from his horse and is sleeping. The stallions of Istęba will whinny, but they will not embark on journeys to Ouhrov. But days and nights once marked by the pallor of death shall end. Peace shall descend and armies shall return.

The clacking and tapping of crutches will resonate outside hospitals and people will flock towards squares.

Hurrah! Hurrah! Hostility is ended, rip up the banners and tear them to shreds with your teeth! Regardless of glory! To spite all captains! The bugle calls and drumbeats that hurled you, already half-dead, into the affray shall no longer be heard. The drum has been run through and the bugle twisted.

Sleep on, Danowitz, your instruments have burned to dust and the roads you traversed shall soon awake to a tumult of another kind. Your times have passed and gone are the colours of hussars. You would have been killed a hundred times over on the path you trod; the times are murderous and you would have been fighting again. Sleep on, Danowitz, you were bedazzled by a world whose demise is imminent. It is coming after you.

Josef will be praying in a madhouse cell, for baronial punishments are horrific. Old Danowitz will not relent while he still has a mite of power, a mite of strength. He had not learned how to forgive. Neither old age nor suffering had left him so woebegone as to make him forget. He is an aristocrat mindful of the code that, for all the fornication and gluttony, does have a kind of nobility, and he will remain one until such time as he is strangled by illness or completely crushed.

Maxmilián returned to Ouhrov; he was alone in the world and the manor was overtaken by nights of contemplation. From cottage to cottage, from door to door, around the houses of labourers partly paid in-kind, something was brewing. Danowitz did not know what. His books remained half-open and words vanished in the silence. Words that had lost all meaning, words that had become a falsehood during the transformations of war.

One day, the Smrdov village priest came to Ouhrov.

"Well, Baron," he said, his hand of a labourer gripping Danowitz's, "how is Josef getting on?"

"Daydreaming," he replied, "dreaming of a journey to Jerusalem and the Kingdom of the poor. I had two sons and they've both died on me."

"To the best of my knowledge," said the priest, "we haven't buried Josef; he's still very much alive, because he is suffering."

"You're speaking his language and maybe you're here on his behalf. Is there something I should do for him?"

"Return him to his rightful estate," said the priest, sitting down in Danowitz's place. "Today every priest and every aristocrat looks mad. What can you expect, Baron? The churches are empty. Things have changed too much, because one day of wartime deprivation is longer than a decade of peace. Your secret, which you have declined to mention, has not been a secret for a long time now. Everybody knows it and everybody talks about it, so, strike the slanderers dumb and have Josef come to Ouhrov."

"The case of the annuity?" Danowitz asked, "I've only ever mentioned it to one man, and he's miles away."

"A mile has become a span in our day and age, now that people travel the length and breadth of the earth."

"But if you were obliged to concede that there is some substance to the matter of the annuity, what would you do then?"

"It would be evidence," said the priest rising, "that Josef is less crazy than I'd thought."

The Smrdov priest left Ouhrov, indignant and enraged.

"I just wonder," he said as he passed by the last of the buildings, "I just wonder if it isn't the intention of justice that this world be razed to the ground. Possibly, since the word of God is mute and emperors are taken for scoundrels, since fathers are tyrants and rebellious sons are defiant and steal, maybe in this confusion over the horrors of war and starvation a new word will hold sway, spelled out by a new faith. Dammit, are we to despair in the end, or be joyful? The Kingdom of the poor was not of this world."

Arrived back at his rectory, the priest closed the breviary that he had left open on his prie-dieu.

"Let this wine be poured out for the welfare of all who shall drink of it. We're old enough, I, Danowitz *and* the Emperor, to be able, as the saying goes, to go to hell. But then, if I were to speak the gospel truth, I was always more peasant than priest and I shall live."

CHAPTER TWELVE

The languages of the world had been trashed into a vulgar hotchpotch of every kind of commonplace, Caesar was snuffing it again and the world's entrails were being devoured by a she-wolf. Songs hollered from the depths, mockery and malediction were giving the god of battles a jouncing, his prolapsed backside agape from a sound kicking, and glory's firmament, shot full of holes, was plummeting down from on high. Soldiers were deserting. At one moment, which arrived with a fearsome rumble, in circles of sparks and to the alarm call of bugles, regiment upon regiment began casting aside their rifles, and troops already almost strangled were in flight. The din and the crackle, the killing and the bloodshed flowing from one end of the world to the other had begun to subside. Cannon still reigned, but the blood-drenched world was rearing up and gaps were appearing in the darkness. A vile crucifixion too large for the eye to encompass, with Golgotha stretching to the ice cap, shook, and the veil of ages was being rent in twain. For the last time, the most terrible things were happening. The world's mane bristled with starvation. Instead of a single spearman, a whole pack assailed the flank of a fellow whose features were turning livid, who had stolen a loaf of bread and who claimed to be a son of man. Scrawny flanks betrayed the rib movements of the starving masses. Woe to the emotionless and dispassionate figurehead that, in flight and over an area consumed by fire, would rule according to the old laws. Cast it into the fire! A burning rat loses its fat at a stroke. For the last time has screaming been heard among so many monstrous voices. Death in the field will seem muted, for the acts and horrors of flight are more terrifying than clashes of arms. Who will be left unscarred by the sword, who will elude the edge of the crescent-curved blade? Be still, thou moment of silence, thou small rock rising above these waters! Float away, ye fulminations of war! In time, no one shall hear any more terrifying tempest played on the instruments of warfare. O, harps of battle! O, fearsome drumbeats and the singing of troops, full of blasphemy and dread, more mighty than the stentorian sea, storm-rent skies and mountains that erupt. O, harps of battle! A tiny child, conceived in the first days of the war, sat silent and bare-legged in the dust of a rubbish heap; it crawled slithering after the soldiers' campfires and in the end, so that a lovely legend might be repeated, it entered the camp on the back of a mule, only remotely reminiscent of a certain little donkey. But the fire sites were black and dead; the child was starving. Teachers who are used to seeing so many strange things have stopped doling out their endless good advice. Fire sites are black and amid the shards of what has been is where continuance lies. Two continents have gone up in flames and for all that fire no one has baked enough bread.

The Gorlice battlefield lay in ruins and the Maytime day was receding. Night was closing in, banishing the ravens – a night of ghosts and of the rattle of death. People half buried in the ground, injured, rousing them-selves like reptiles and devils who've taken a hiding, faces hellish and weeping, and, again, headless bodies, limbless trunks, bones, the offal and scraps of armies, body upon body, dead upon living, they waited for wolf or dog to come out of its hiding place, squat on its haunches and gnaw and lick at their wounds. Right up until dawn, through the day and another night this host will be gasping for breath like ghastly fish that someone has hooked and then cast upon this field. No droplet of dew will seep onto their lips, they will thirst, cry out for water, for a sponge soaked in vinegar and for the gall tendered to Jesus Christ. A flock of crows will drop down at daybreak. Sighing and moaning, growing faint-er by the hour, will no longer scare them. All has been dashed and turned to naught. All has been trampled down and done for. And yet! From these seeds sown shall rise young shoots and a turbulent forest that shall surge up and inflame the world, meridian by meridian, parallel by parallel.

The tempests have flown and their pinions now shade the rural scene.

The men of the medical corps, who had been seeking the perquisites of their trade and, having tarried for three days, found them, arrived in those parts around Mościska well-fed on the rations of the dead. They could chat as at other times, arrange matters between them and they were in high spirits, because the fighting had ceased.

"Hey," said one soldier, holding up a helmet full of ashes, "doesn't it look as if this infantryman was playing games, carrying fire in his pot?"

"He wasn't playing any more than we do, carrying water," another replied.

"Right then, let's get down to work."

They separated the dead from the living, like unto ravens or Shakespeare's gravediggers.

František Řeka was lifted and carried away, unconscious. Having no mouth, he could not drink, and the soldier who from habit put a bottle to his lips withdrew his hand in horror.

"God!" he exclaimed, "how can he still be alive! What's his name? Who is it?"

They unbuttoned his tunic.

"What have you done with your shirt? Where's the holder with your name tag?"

"Wait," said a passing corporal, "wait till he runs out of patience, then he might show you. Can't you see he's all bled out and his tongue's missing?"

They inserted a kind of gag in his mouth, compressed his carotid artery with a bandage folded into a billet, placed him on a stretcher and order two Jews to take him away.

Řeka came to; the Ouhrov grange was coming to its ploughman as in a dream. He saw a high and bright sky, cattle and a cluster of wagons. What day was this coming? He felt as if he were drunk and as if Lei was coming to thrash him. He tried to shout and gushed blood.

"Put him down. To the dressing station!" said a doctor, almost beside himself in the deluge of blood, which had soaked him from top to toe. "Oh dear," he exhaled, not having time to say much, "what am I to do?" Finally, device in hand, he bent over the wretched head, which was howling with laughter.

"Over here," he said, leaving. "Pour some brandy down that funnel. He's dying! Hurry up!"

Bandaged and with the doctor's device in his throat, Řeka fell asleep. They loaded him onto a wagon, or rather slung his stretcher to the straps on it, and it flailed about like a ship at sea. A driver took the reins and drove across a trackless field. At eventide they stopped at some shattered village. The agony, still masked by his semi-conscious state, ran through Řeka's sorry frame, touching all his extremities. He woke up and objects hurtled like animals towards his sorry gaze. He saw a tree sway as it approached him. He saw a gun carriage with its wheels turning and its shaft pointing at his forehead. Crows were flying out of the mountains towards him and an odd flock emerged and vanished before him as if he had devoured it. It was an old Friday. Within the dilapidated walls of the Smrdov church its illustrious bell stirred, and the crowd given to hanging about at patronal feasts headed for the poor retainer. Hello there! Hello! František Řeka, who owes no one anything, who pays his debts! Make way for him! Make way, let him through! He will scare you as he gawks into the carbine barrels that you have raised. He will scare you with the bloody mask that he has attached to his face, he will scare you, then take it off again, for it unpins like a wedding ribbon.

The journey continued, at one point a soldier stepped up to the stretcher and a cheery voice could be heard, so familiar from the old days. Inside Řeka's head a tongue of fire stirred, capable of responding to any halloo.

"It's a good day today."

"Good day."

Ah, the words are stars that ignite in the dark firmament of the mind. Words so familiar. Words from the old days! I'd give all the baron's money, all Lei's possessions for a single cry: Ouhrov! For he who is speaking knows me, he would rush to my aid, he would take me by the hand and recognise that I am František Řeka, an old Ouhrov retainer. He might say just one little word more, he might take me into his arms and he might carry me out into the middle of the yard where the wagons stand in a line and where the animal shed is. A shed filled with lowing, oxen with chaplets of hair, beautiful eyes, solid horns and breath that rises in a column when it's freezing cold. O, Ouhrov! O, garden so green!

František made to rise and, lifting back the clasp of the strap, he tapped on the bar that held the wagon's cover, tapped endlessly until, his strength having failed him, he passed out.

On the box, the Ouhrov soldier with the ginger moustache was chatting to the driver with no inkling that František Řeka was calling to him from inside the wagon.

"They've been disastrous times," he said, "but I found what I was looking for, I've got a fairly plausible and heroic injury, having shot myself in the right hand with a Russian bullet. I was a while thinking about it, because things like that carry a penalty."

"But of course, if some idiot shoots himself in such a way that he's left with a burn mark from his rifle muzzle and the bullet shoots straight downwards through his thigh, and if they find grains of powder in the wound, it'll usually go bad for him, but then who would be so stupid!"

The Ouhrov soldier said: "I fired through a loaf of bread, which they say is the best dust trap."

Meanwhile, the wagon had passed through the battle zone. They'd met soldiers who were camped in villages and occupying the cottages.

"How are you getting on? You chaps know how to lounge about! It's not that hard to keep an eye out for aeroplanes and practically have breakfast in bed! Strewth, round here you'll hear gunfire barely once in a blue moon!"

Finally they reached the dressing station. The Ouhrov soldier hopped off the wagon and, taking the head end, lifted František's stretcher with the injured man staring into his face and calling out his name without a sound.

"Ugh," said the soldier, gazing at Řeka's heavenward stare, "this is some injury! The man's lost half his head!"

František's name, the name Řeka, pure lyricism on the part of some official, who had thought long before hitting on it, this lyricism had been forgotten. Ignorant of writing and being beyond all recognition, the injured man could but nod in response to questions. Along with his image, his name was lost.

An NCO brought in a piece of paper and František made two crosses, lacking the strength to make a third.

It began to rain and the procession moved on. Soldiers black and menacing stood in huddles, the wind tugged at their capes and the rain soaked them through. But the wagons of the injured kept moving, lurching towards some hell, and the rain drummed on their tilts. Two streams, as if the world were split in twain, like west and east, brushing against each other, edge to edge, went their way. It looked as if forests were on the march.

Wagons, cannon, frothing horses, a host, an assembly, a kind of infernal camp, noise, tramping, rattling, roaring, voices, everything benumbed, everything rushing with spastic tread and shifting weight, faces on top of the capes of a force wedged in a chasm of confusion, made their way forward in two directions. Two obscurities, two horrors no longer bound by feasance, had embarked on their way.

The wagon of the dying, the eeriest of all in this procession of phantoms, was hauled by day and by night all the way to the railhead. Herds of engines and whole townships of trucks and carriages, the one-time backwater had become the hellhole from which these streams had gushed and through which they were now returning; it had been a gateway to conflagration and was become a gateway to tranquillity. Here, along with the others, they set František down on the ground.

Again he could see the vast expanse of the empyrean and scan a sky almost worthy of Ouhrov, for springtime had once more cloaked this war. František kept tapping the name he had lost on the frame of his stretcher. He stutters no more and is silent. He is no longer a man, but a mystery, whose countenance is his wound. His name lies forgotten in the firmament of the poor. All he is is his injury. He will die at the military hospital in Prague, making three crosses on a piece of white paper, for he never learned to write and used to be a simpleton.

Who is this? A hero. A hero who fell and is silent. A madman raving with all the terrifying eloquence inside his head.

Six soldiers will take up his coffin and bear it through the city centre, and fire and smoke will spout in his honour from the barrels of army rifles. A salvo will be fired. The bier will be led by a drummer and a black-clad rider with a banner, for, after the manner of all wars, it is occasionally required to conduct with due solemnity the burial of an unknown warrior. An unknown warrior who died in an enigmatic silence at just the right moment, sparing them the bother of his onward conveyance.

A general, one who has done very nicely out of ravaging library after library and stately home after stately home, marches alongside the coffin, musing on his dealings, and all those there with him have their minds on their affairs, cursing the ceremony for dragging on so.

To hell with your unknown warrior and ceremonies that call for no binoculars! To hell with tears, to hell with war! The spectre is unmantled, laid bare! Lo, a skeleton counting out his money amid a deluge of fire! Lo, a city roused from slumber and pointing at a nocturnal apparition divested of all charm!

March on, procession, raise the banner high, sound your trumpets! Glory embraced in a daze vanishes and passes from custom. The dominion of wars is done for. Thousands of enemies arise from their hellholes of hunger to frustrate its passage. It has required nothing less than the killing of people and putting the tormented countenance of corpses on view. It has required naught but to cleanse the seats of fire of the scoria of glory for armies to choke on the smoke and be burned up in geysers of fire.

Imperial armies have been turned into a mob and the rabble roams the suburbs, making a mockery of the grim shortages. These men are long of face, clad in the chequered attire of jesters, squawking and hissing their imprecations in the vernacular native to army life. Their shorn smile has long lacked any trace of the bristly laughter of a man given to guffawing whenever he has a moment. Army-issue leg wraps still adorn their shins. They bear all the marks that define the other side of wars: the hand of the petty thief, the mountebank's shoulders, the money-grubber's wad and syphilis. Their words, peeled away from objects, mangled and devoid of all sense, jingle and hiss and clatter as if tongues were tipsy.

A rank of these laggards, augmented by crowds of women, lined the house-fronts along the streets taken by the funeral cortège.

František was borne through the midst of this assemblage, passing through it as a Mardi Gras parade passes through Nice. Six men from different arms marched beneath him and a grand tailpiece of generals and provincial governors trudged along in the coffin's wake. They had raised a nameless one above all names, and above all heads they had, as befits wars, raised a madman.

The procession was headed by a tattoo of drums. Drums a-drubbing. Drums of derision.

The wars have been lost. Haul along the killer of Ouhrov whom you've stolen, haul him, you corpse thieves, haul him, the wars are lost! You have taught nations to speak the language of the rabble. You have taught them to blight all work and impair all health. You have shaken the money boxes of the poor and gathered up the scattered small change. You shall be felled by the axe that *you* sharpened, and the shots *you* discharged shall end lodged inside *you*. May the old world perish, may it turn belly-up, may new things arise in urban wastelands, and may the broad, trackless expanse of the steppe contract into a single highway.

Halt, ye hosts, before the unknown warrior! May he pass through you as through a gaping gate. Scoff ye at the generals and governors, scoff and spit upon the road they tread. Vent ye your scorn on depilated glory, but bide ye in silence for František as he hastens to his grave. He was a murderer, but he has been forgiven, he was a death-dealing blade, but one now melted down.

A wind blew into the crackling fires and the earth, having been opened up slightly, spilled back into place. František Řeka had been buried.

"Let him sleep." said a man standing at a street corner, "why bang on the coffin? Let him lie in his grave, he's done for and it were *them* as stuffed 'im. That's why the march of the tenth round of draftees won't stop now. War's not going to lose sleep on his account. Bah! Go get yourself an injury that won't exceed ten months and isn't short on fun. Go get your share, artfully and like a thief. Drink of the wine barrels of Italy and bring home five chemises for your whores, for in war you steal and don't get killed."

"Get yourself taken captive," said someone else, and a third, who'd heard about the Czech force, could wish for nothing more than to be among them.

Things of the past are ceasing to be. All that has been great has been made small, fires are the work of arsonists, the executioner's axe has been made a mockery, all bread has been eaten and the bludgeoned heads of nations are dipping towards their shoulders.

The day of labour dawns, a star and a new era, for the years shall be counted from the war's end, as from the dawn of creation.

Year one, two, three, up to thousands!

Wars shall fall through a mesh of gossamer. The age of dominion has been smashed and the age of the workers is beginning. Like mountains and seas, fire and blood shall separate the two periods. You used to make haste as you turned the soil, sowed and reaped, like a god you created cities and like a silkworm silk, but your labour has been purloined and the cry for bread has not fallen silent for a single second. So from this point, from this abyss, from the peaks of war a new crusade is beginning, a sweeping, a most glorious campaign of labour.

Wars are a lost cause. The bugle call is become pure swagger, the voice of revolt and the impulse to rebel are astir within every man. One time, around mid-summer, you had been damned keen on amassing enough togs for winter camp. You gave men plenty to drink and called them by their Christian names. You yourselves rammed army caps on their heads, but now you have come to your senses and the times have changed. You know what to say to those seeking out deserters in granaries. You have learned to be true and naught now stands in the way of your entering upon a brand-new age, but for one thing. But for the cant of the rabble.

The real idiom of workers is labour.

The loam that barely covers the porphyry, gneiss and schist about the middle reaches of the River Vltava, the shallow topsoil with a smidgen of clay on the western slopes of some hills that have no name, the depths of ordinariness, the floor of destitution, is by no means so meagre for woods not to have sprung from it. They do spring, exactly as speech – before being rendered at last by a voice – springs over the course of a long silence.

The old generation of workers and new arrivals on

the scene will be stirred to revolt beneath blows and lashings, the coppery cloud of calm blown wide open in a flash.

The barrier of destitution has been smashed and the cramped spot is becoming a wide-open space. It shall be traversed by blithesome pathways from north to south and from east to west. Time, oscillating this way and that like a pendulum, has been swept away by the terrible motion of war. The veil of the temple has been rent in twain and the age of the Old Testament is at an end. The world has been circumnavigated and criss-crossed by expeditions and the shadow of knowledge does not block out the mind of Ouhrov. The lions in the borderlands have died the death. The manor house at Ouhrov, a terror-stricken edifice on a hillock that goes by the name of Noonday Witch, is going to rack and ruin, and a carter, barely bothering to turn that way, will point to its turrets with the tip of his whip. The class of the Danowitzes has been given a hiding, gone mad and will be reduced to beggary. Merchants shall choke on their change. Were it not for the commonwealths of workers, the world would be desolate. May the songs bellowed from the depths, the deriding, the cursing and the dreadful mischief-making all fall silent. May the world's bristling mane lie flat, may the Golgotha that stretches to the ice cap be razed, may nothing of the past set foot beyond the first summer. The last soldier of the

Great War, a killer who never went on trial, is straining to hear. His face tiger-striped by worms and his wound weeping, he stares upwards, waiting for the mound of glory raised over his grave to be razed to the ground.

TRANSLATOR'S NOTES

p. 1 *Many peoples shall come and say, "Come, let us go up to the moun-*
tain of the Lord, to the house of the God of Jacob; that he may teach
us his ways and that we may walk in his paths." For out of Zion shall
go forth instruction, and the word of the Lord from Jerusalem. He
shall judge between the nations, and shall arbitrate for many peo-
ples; they shall beat their swords into ploughshares, and their spears
into pruning hooks; nation shall not lift up sword against nation,
neither shall they learn war any more. – Isaiah 2:3–4

The original title of Vančura's remarkable anti-war novel is,
in structural terms, the very antithesis of Isaiah's optimistic
prognosis. *Pole orná a válečná* reads literally as 'Fields arable
and of war'.

Many friends and colleagues gave thought to how to deal
with this knotty problem, an intermediate solution being
to borrow and invert Isaiah's swords and ploughshares, as
'shares and swords' – the near-alliteration being some com-
pensation for the duality of the original.

The English Wikipedia page *Swords to ploughshares* tells us that
the underlying Hebrew word *'êt* also means 'coulter', which
led at one stage to the suggestion that the translation might
be headed *Coulters into Carbines*, the carbine being very much
in evidence in World War I and also earning the odd mention
in Vančura's text. However, the notion of ploughshares being
beaten into swords (swords also feature quite often in the
novel) was finally agreed as most properly echoing the Isaiah
text. Vančura himself surely had Isaiah in mind.

For Vančura it would not, of course, be the Lord who would
judge among the nations and engineer everlasting peace by
turning swords back into ploughshares, but, at the opposite
end of the scale, the revolutionary, international proletariat,
the rustic element of which had indeed seen, *inter alia*, the farm
equipment that it worked by hand turned into weaponry –

including such hand-held items as the swords and sabres of the swanky officer class.

p. 42   The single-beam scaling ladder is a common device on old Bohemian coats-of-arms, less commonly also seen in Germany. It symbolised valour.

p. 48   The *Sovereign Military Order of Malta, officially the Sovereign Military Hospitaller Order of Saint John of Jerusalem, of Rhodes and of Malta*, widely referred to as the *Order of Malta*, is a Catholic lay religious order, traditionally with military, chivalric and aristocratic associations. It has been called "the smallest sovereign state in the world", though not recognised as such by the United Nations. The Order claims continuity with the *Knights Hospitallers,* an order of chivalry founded c. 1099 by the Blessed Gerard in Jerusalem. Later references in the novel to an 'order of knighthood' or similar will refer to this same body.

p. 59   For one account of this probably Romano-British saint and the 11,000 of her followers massacred at Cologne for failing to oblige the Huns sexually see https://www.historic-uk .com/HistoryUK/HistoryofEngland/Saint-Ursula-the-11000 -British-Virgins/. The Victoria & Albert Museum houses a magnificently gory fifteenth-century painting of a twelfth-century version of the legend.

p. 61   Vác St. (Váci utca) is the main thoroughfare (now pedestrianised) running north from central Budapest. It runs parallel to the Danube and starts from the parish of St Theresa of Ávila, whose church lies some way to the south-east.

p. 105 A green wreath of vine leaves was widely used as part of or alongside inn signs. Many hostelries in the Czech Republic are still called The Green Wreath.

p. 114 There is in Galicia no actual place called Przegonina at any major crossroads which Josef may be assumed to have passed through; the name is as fictitious as all the little Ouhrovs, Smrdovs, Istębas and so on, in contrast to the larger, non-fictitious cities encountered in the novel, such as Buda(pest), Vienna or Cracow and, possibly, Hradec. However, as it will transpire later in the book, Vančura's knowledge of the war in Galicia is hugely detailed. Today's Lemko village of Bodaki – just north of the frontier with Slovakia – has, by administrative changes – swallowed up the erstwhile hamlet of Przegonina nearby, which is now recalled only in the name of War Cemetery No. 69, where 55 Austrians and 74 Russians were buried following a battle that took place there on 3 May 1915. One might surmise that the name simply stuck in Vančura's mind and was then found suitable for re-use here.

p. 119 It is worth remembering, here as elsewhere, that 'Hungary' at the time meant the Hungarian half of the Austro-Hungarian Empire and embraced what we know today as Slovakia, Sub-Carpathian Ruthenia, Croatia and Transylvania as well as Hungary *sensu stricto*.

p. 127 Jabůrek: The 'hero' of a popular, anonymous song about the Battle of Sadowa (Sadová, Königgrätz; 3 July 1866) during the Austro-Prussian War. The Prussian victory practically brought the war to an end, though there were a few more skirmishes up to July 22. In the song, Jabůrek stands firmly beside his cannon, loading and reloading it non-stop.

p. 129 Emperor Franz Joseph I of Austria signed a mobilization order for eight army corps to begin operations against Serbia within 72 hours, while Austro-Hungarian ambassador Baron Wladimir Giesl von Gieslingen left Belgrade. (Fritz Fischer: *Germany's Aims in the First World War*. New York: W.W. Norton, 1967, p. 67)

p. 129 Heinrich Leonhard von Tschirschky und Bögendorff (1858–1916), German ambassador to Austria.

p. 132 Horodenka: A town in Galicia held by Austria until 1918, then by Poland until 1939. The Jewish population had reached 36 per cent in 1900 and continued to rise to *c.* 50

per cent, the mass destruction of whom at the hands of the Ukrainian majority and Nazi invaders in World War II was one of the more egregious manifestations of the Holocaust. Its name is remembered at a Hebrew congregation in Salford, England.

p. 133 Albert Theodor Otto Emmich (from 1913 von Emmich) (1848–1915), a Prussian general noted for his special unit's task of taking the forts at Liège to clear the way for the regular German army.

p. 133 *Jeder Stoß ein Franzos!*: This slogan was one of four: *Jeder Schuß ein Russ, Jeder Stoß ein Franzos, Jeder Tritt ein Britt, Jeder Klaps ein Japs*, as used, for example, on a period propaganda postcard, widely described on the internet.

p. 133 *Zum Frühstück auf nach Paris!*: Another period slogan, recently (1990) given new life in a popular song by Oliver Frank (b. 1963).

p. 136 Gyula: A town in SE Hungary, today close to the Romanian frontier.

p. 138 'Lift not up your horns' – from Psalm 75.

p. 138 'Blow ye the trumpet...' In the context, this carries a strong echo of Joel 2:1.

p. 138 'not one stone has been left on another', as foreseen in Mark 13:2.

p. 148 St Catherine's Day, i.e. 25 November, rather late.

p. 153 Francis, i.e. Francis (Franz) Joseph I, Austro-Hungarian emperor until 1916.

p. 162 Alfred Graf von Schlieffen (1833–1913), German field marshal and military strategist who served as chief of the Imperial German General Staff from 1891 to 1906. German planning for the conduct of WWI was named posthumously after him, as the Schlieffen Plan.

p. 163 The Innocents: possibly a reference to the Battles of Ypres and the *Kindermord* – Massacre of the Innocents, a corps of very young German reservists. French (and Belgian and British) losses were also very high.

p. 164 Paul Georg Edler von Rennenkampff (1854–1918 [executed by the Bolsheviks]), known in English as Paul von Rennenkampf, was a Baltic-German nobleman and general of the Russian imperial army, v. https://en.wikipedia.org/wiki/Paul _von_Rennenkampf for a partial explanation of why Vančura calls him traitorous.

p. 164 Aleksandr Vasilyevich Samsonov (1859–1914 [suicide]) was a career officer in the cavalry of the Imperial Russian Army and a general during the Russo-Japanese War and World War I, v. https://en.wikipedia. org/wiki/Alexander_Samsonov.

p. 164 Wirhallen is not on any map. Possibly hinting at today's Vilkaviškis, Lithuania, just east of the border with what was East Prussia, though that was actually called *Wilkowischken* in German.

p. 164 Insterburg and Goldap, two towns just inside East Prussia, today Chernyakovsk in Russia's Kaliningrad exclave, and Goldap in northern Poland.

p. 164 Alexander Heinrich Rudolph von Kluck (1846–1934), a German general during World War I.

p. 164 Paul Ludwig Hans Anton von Beneckendorff und von Hindenburg, known simply as (Paul von) Hindenburg (1847–1934), was a German general (for a time in command of cavalry regiments) and statesman who commanded the Imperial German Army during World War I and later became President of Germany from 1925 until his death.

p. 165 Allenstein, i.e. Olsztyn in today's Poland. This is an account of the Battle of Tannenberg, one of the earliest encounters of World War I, in which the Russians were roundly defeated. It was named by Hindenburg after Tannenberg further to the west, as revenge for the Teutonic Knights' crushing defeat by Poland-Lithuania 500 years previously at the Battle of Grunwald, itself once known to Germans as the Battle of Tannenberg.

p. 166 Jiaozhou on China's Shandong Peninsula, at the time part of the Jiaozhou Bay territory, leased by Germany (cf. Britain's lease of Hong Kong), its name romanised as Kiaochow, Kiauchau or Kiao-Chau in English and as Kiautschou or Kiaochau in German.

p. 166 Tsingtao, now spelled Qingdao, the spelling Tsingtao – especially in the context of the German-style beer it has produced – looks back to the city's 'colonial' past and the Japanese Siege of Tsingtao (or Tsingtau) in 1914. It was the capital of the territory leased to Germany.

p. 167 Erzherzog Joseph Ferdinand Habsburg (1872–1942), whose military career later suffered such setbacks that not even membership of the royal family could save him from disgrace. In later life he became the only Habsburg to see the inside of a concentration camp. See http://www.austro-hungarian-army.co.uk/biog/josferd.htm.

p. 167 Eduard Freiherr von Böhm-Ermolli (1856–1941), Austrian general during World War I who rose to the rank of field marshal in the Austro-Hungarian Army. His army had been on the Serbian front but when Russia entered the war it was moved north for the action in Galicia.

p. 167 The generalised Battle of Galicia consisted of a number of distinct engagements, including the Battle of Rawa on 3–11 September, 1914.

p. 176 Which von Bülow (with only one -l-) is meant is unclear; General Karl of that ilk was busy losing the Battle of the Marne at the time, and I have found no other candidate.

p. 176 Mishchenko possibly refers to Pavel Ivanovich Mishchenko (1853–1918), a career military officer of the Imperial Russian Army and statesman of Ukrainian ethnicity.

p. 176 Grajewo, a small town in NE Poland, occupied during World War I first by Russia then by the Germans.

p. 178 Dobrovolsk, called *Pillkallen*, in Polish *Piłkały*, from 1510 to 1938 and *Schloßberg* from 1938 to 1947, a village in East Prussia, now in the Krasnoznamensky District of Russia's Kaliningrad exclave.

p. 179 Somossy Orpheum, also known as the Operetta Theatre in Budapest, a fine Art nouveau structure built in 1894.

p. 199 Brothers of Mercy, formally known as the Brothers Hospitallers of Saint John of God, an order still active worldwide.

p. 207 Radetzky, in full Johann Josef Wenzel Anton Franz Karl, Graf Radetzky von Radetz (Czech: *Jan Josef Václav Antonín František Karel hrabě Radecký z Radče*; 1766–1858), Bohemian aristocrat and Austrian field marshal. He was chief of the Habsburg Monarchy's general staff during the later period of the Napoleonic Wars. A disciplinarian, but fair, he was well liked by his troops. He is renowned for his victories at the Battles of Custoza (24–25 July 1848) and Novara (23 March 1849) during the First Italian War of Independence, and is remembered in Johann Strauss's *Radetzky March*, commissioned to commemorate the victory at Custoza.

The Battle of Solferino (June 24, 1859) was the last engagement of the Second War of Italian Independence, waged in Lombardy between the Austrians and the French in alliance with the Piedmontese. Austria was defeated with the result that most of Lombardy was annexed by Sardinia-Piedmont, one stage in the unification of Italy. Radetzky had been dead for 17 months.

p. 222 Today's Gorlice is in Poland. The reference is to the Gorlice-Tarnów Offensive of May/June 1915, a major military success for Austria-Hungary and Germany on the Eastern Front. Following the joint campaign of the Central Powers, the Russian army had to beat a retreat along a wide front and was neutralised as a fighting force for months to come. See https://encyclopedia.1914-1918-online.net/article/offensive_gorlice-tarnow.

p. 223 Field Marshal Anton Ludwig Friedrich August von Mackensen (1849–1945), the hugely successful commander of the joint German and Austro-Hungarian armies in the Galician campaign and later. For more on his life and military career see, for example, https://www.britannica.com/biography/August-von-Mackensen, or https://en.wikipedia.org/wiki/August_von_Mackensen.

p. 224 Mościska, possibly the town now called Mostyska, in the Ukraine, previously in Galicia and still having a Polish minority.

p. 227 Today there is a hospital in St Lazarus Street, Cracow, though it does not carry the saint's name. Moreover it lies south-east of the city centre, not on the north-eastern fringes.

p. 257 The Czech force, i.e. those who had defected to the Russians.

The most famous Czech contribution to world literature about the Great War is Jaroslav Hašek's *The Good Soldier Švejk* (1923), which established Czech literature's international reputation for humorous pub anecdotes and tales of plucky underdogs playfully subverting unjust and overweening authority. One can only wonder how differently that reputation might have developed if Vladislav Vančura's *Ploughshares into Swords* (1925) had been translated in the late 1920s. Its brooding intensity and preoccupation with degeneration and death, combining features of Naturalism, Decadence and Expressionism, recall the fin-de-siècle writing that Vančura admired in his youth. At the same time, its monumentally constructed prose, memorably described by the poet František Halas as 'somewhere between a psalm and a hymn', reflects the pervasive influence of the Baroque worldview and imagery in modern Czech writing.

In fact, it is unlikely that this novel was high on anyone's list for translation in 1925. Many reviewers struggled with its remorseless darkness, the fractured plotlines and the absence of attractive characters or any sense of optimism, which seemed to belong to an earlier period. Over fifty years later, one prominent commentator admitted that Czech critics and readers had yet to come to terms with the work. These days, Vančura is best known among Czech readers for his self-consciously much lighter next novel, *The Summer of Caprice* (1926), also published by the Karolinum Press in the Modern Czech Classics series, and the stylized medieval romance, *Markéta Lazarová* (1930), both of which were successfully filmed in the 1960s. He is also justly remembered for the chronicle of Bohemian history that he began publishing to strengthen the resolve of the occupied Czechs during the

Second World War, a project cut short when he was arrested and executed by the Germans in 1942 for suspected involvement in the Communist resistance. For a few reviewers at the time and since, however, *Ploughshares into Swords* constitutes his greatest literary achievement and one of the most distinctive and radical in all Czech literature.

Vančura belongs to the same generation as the most internationally successful Czech writer of the period, Karel Čapek, but only began publishing in earnest in the 1920s. Franz Kafka, in a rare comment on contemporary Czech-language literature, wrote favourably about one of his early short stories. In his work, Vančura expresses a far more ambitious and uncompromising vision of literature than Čapek. To some extent, he found kindred spirits in the much younger left-wing Avant-garde poets like Vítězslav Nezval (1900–57), with whom he founded the most famous Czech Avant-garde grouping, Devětsil, in 1920. His writing, however, rarely reflects their proto-Surrealist, Poetist aesthetic; he pokes fun at their love of circuses and acrobats in *The Summer of Caprice*, and from his first novel – and most strikingly in *Ploughshares into Swords* – he focuses like Proletarian writers on labour, the community of the marginalized, and the grinding misery of working-class poverty and inequality. A recurring technique of his writing, however, is the discrepancy between the often stagnant, grim or mundane realities of the lives of his characters and the language he uses to describe it. More than any other novelist, he ostentatiously explores the depth and variety of the Czech language, excavating its lexical, grammatical and syntactical memory. His dynamic interweaving of scriptural and early modern Czech, the language of geography, geology, historiography, the sciences and trades, and the poetry of colloquial language serves as a metaphor for the potential suppressed in the human being in contemporary society.

It would be wrong to suggest that Czech critics were not equipped to appreciate the horizons of modernism attained in *Ploughshares into Swords*, but most did not seek or anticipate them in their own literature. Its closest counterpart stylistically in Czech literature is the devastating short-story cycle *The Furies* (1918) by Richard Weiner (1884–1937), based on his experiences in the war. Unlike the 'legionary literature' written by Czech soldiers who experienced the campaigns on the eastern front and the Russian Civil War, it is not an eye-witness account founded on Realist approaches. Vančura did not see action in the First World War, but asserts the ability of the artistic imagination to capture something essential about conflict without having experienced it first-hand. His novel also lacks the patriotism and sentimentality typical of the legionaries' novels. The ambition and vision of Vančura's novel more closely resemble inter-war Russian and American writing about war, poverty and social upheaval. Like early post-revolutionary Russian experimental fiction, *Ploughshares into Swords* privileges the portrayal of chaos over rebirth, and frequently revives the techniques and imagery of Symbolism. In common with Boris Pilnyak's *The Naked Year* (1922), it captures through fragmentation the final throes of a corrupt and discredited social order, though without any hint among the cast of characters of the spirit or values that will define the better world to come. With Isaak Babel's *Red Cavalry* (1926) it shares a sense of the bloody chaos, futility and absurdity of military conflict, though with fewer of Babel's warmer comic interludes. Perhaps paradoxically, Vančura's approach to portraying society in late Austria-Hungary resonates most clearly, however, with Andrei

Platonov's comparably bleak, radically defamiliarized satire of early Stalinism in *The Foundation Pit* (completed in 1930).

The English-language writer whose style comes closest to the Vančura of *Ploughshares into Swords* is probably William Faulkner. An English-speaking reader seeking an authentic sense of how Vančura's narration sounds might also compare its opening description of the novel's setting to that of John Steinbeck's later *The Grapes of Wrath* (1939), which is strikingly similar in style:

> To the red country and part of the gray country of Oklahoma, the last rains came gently, and they did not cut the scarred earth. The plows crossed and recrossed the rivulet marks. The last rains lifted the corn quickly and scattered weed colonies and grass along the sides of the roads so that the gray country and the dark red country began to disappear under a green cover. In the last part of May the sky grew pale and the clouds that had hung in high puffs for so long in the spring were dissipated. The sun flared down on the growing corn day after day until a line of brown spread along the edge of each green bayonet. The clouds appeared, and went away, and in a while they did not try any more. The weeds grew darker green to protect themselves, and they did not spread any more. The surface of the earth crusted, a thin hard crust, and as the sky became pale, so the earth became pale, pink in the red country and white in the gray country.

Steinbeck presents the Great Depression in apocalyptic terms, established by the reference to the Book of Revelation in his title. Vančura likewise characterizes the First World War in *Ploughshares into Swords* as the end of one world and the birth of another. His title reverses the Old Testament prophecy: 'and they shall beat their swords into ploughshares' (Isaiah 2:4, also Micah 4:3), which may lead the reader to expect a contrast between the pastoral idyll of farming and the horror of war. In the novel, however, Vančura presents the outbreak of the First World War not as an anomalous interruption, but as the logical continuation of the ghastly violence and hardship experienced by impoverished peasants on the land. Unlike Steinbeck, Vančura provides no anti-heroic image of noble humanity, struggling in vain against the system.

Perhaps the key mistake made by early reviewers of *Ploughshares into Swords* was to read the novel as a work of Naturalism, not only because that style would seem anachronistic in the 1920s, but also because, read through this frame, the exclusively negative portrayal of human beings and behaviour appears unbalanced, exaggerated and unrealistic. Vančura's novel is better understood as a prose-poem, a grotesque Expressionist epic of self-inflicted human torment, designed to provoke a visceral, outraged reaction in its audience. The form is determined by the content and message of the novel. Vančura intertwines the stories of the peasants and landowners on what is effectively still a feudal estate not to highlight the contrast between rich and poor, but to show how similar they are, how the social relations that are plunging everyone into the abyss of war have deformed all involved. The dismal, rotten estate serves as a metaphor perhaps for Bohemia, for Austria-Hungary or for Europe. The plot threads peter out, end bathetically or remain unresolved not because of the author's incompetence, but because in this wretched place, no plan can ever succeed, but always ends in crass, distorted humiliation, whether the murder plans of Švejk's barely recognizable counterpart, the half-witted orphan-peasant Řeka, or the equally ineffectual aristocrat-seminarian Josef Danowitz's plans to travel to Jerusalem.

The narration proceeds in fragments that the reader has to piece together to reflect perhaps a world shattered by war, or perhaps the total breakdown of human community and empathy that pre-dates the war. It is the reader who notices the parallels between characters' actions and fates; the characters themselves, reduced to animal-like existences, are aware of one another in only basic ways. The lack of positive human collective life is encapsulated in the absence of love, whether between men and women, comrades in work or at arms, or father and son. Vančura portrays sexual intercourse not as an expression of love or the desire to procreate, but as either a desperate attempt by those near death to feel alive, or a futile waste of male aggression that might be better channelled into violent rebellion. The absence of any significant female characters is unusual for Vančura, for whom women often embody the love, vitality and inner strength that are lacking in their male counterparts; it reflects a world in which these qualities are missing, and which is doomed to extinction. This prognosis is made clear in the first chapter, in which Vančura, a medical doctor by training, concludes the painful story of Hora's short-lived marriage with the horrific autopsy report produced following the botched delivery that kills both his wife and baby.

In her memoirs, Vančura's wife, Ludmila, recalls his frustration that, thanks to the reception of *Ploughshares into Swords*, he became known as a 'poet of destruction and terror'. In his writing, he repeatedly returns to the 1910s, the implicit period of transition from Austria to Czechoslovakia, in which the world war acted as the fire that destroyed the old world and wrought the new. As a quintessential Modernist, he positions himself on the threshold of crisis and change; the utopian future always takes the form of hints and visions. In *Ploughshares into Swords*, a priest predicts to

Baron Danowitz that a new faith will sweep away the aristocracy and Christianity, and wonders whether perhaps even they will have cause to rejoice. Travelling east towards what Vančura always portrays as a region less corrupted by government and money, Josef Danowitz encounters a tramp, a road-mender and a peasant, examples of the merry, often homeless social outsiders whom Vančura celebrates in his work, and their unthinking comradeship offers a contrasting model of human existence to Josef's crippling, self-centred alienation and self-pity. At the end of the novel, Řeka dies on a Friday in a battle explicitly compared to Golgotha. For Vančura, there could be no more fitting emblem of the hypocritical era now passed, the era that created Řeka as it failed him, than that such a wretched, unheroic figure should serve as the model for the statue of the unknown soldier. The comparison with Christ is not, however, only ironic; the sacrifice of Řeka and millions like him, not in war but in the daily misery of their lives, has inspired the salvation and resurrection of humanity.

Hope in *Ploughshares into Swords* derives ultimately from the strength and confidence of the narrating voice, which embodies the author's vision of a more powerful, liberated humanity, utterly different from the feeble and devastated characters it describes. Vančura's narrator, like the traditional epic narrator, sets scenes and evokes atmospheres, he reports, mocks, condemns, pities, elicits the reader's opinion, advises the reader what to think and takes rhetorical flight. His mastery and freedom contrast absolutely with the verbal incoherence that Řeka exhibits throughout the book in his thoughts and interactions, which is actualized when the lower part of his face is blown off in battle. In the final pages of the novel, Vančura declares that with the coming of the new world, those who have previously been silenced will find their voice.

For an English-speaking reader today, to read *Ploughshares into Swords* is to transport oneself back to not only a different time, space and historical experience, but also to a different worldview and understanding of art. Vančura inherited from the Czech writers of the 1890s a fierce scepticism that what he perceived as bloodless, superficially conservative Czech petty bourgeois society could generate and sustain profound, meaningful artistic or political change, and he sought with *Ploughshares into Swords* to inject anger, passion and ambition into both contexts. Through its portrayal of the antithesis of the ideal, it exemplifies his faith in not only a more just and generous world, but also art as an instrument of awakening and transformation. Especially since the 1960s, high literature has largely ceded the epic perspective to cinema, an emerging art form that fascinated Vančura, who turned his hand to directing films in the 1930s. *Ploughshares into Swords*, however, is an assertion of what only literature can do, an anti-*Iliad*, bereft of heroes and glory, but through its narrator imbued with confidence that, individually and collectively, human beings can be much more.

Rajendra Chitnis
University College, Oxford

ABOUT THE AUTHOR

VLADISLAV VANČURA (1891–1942) was an author, playwright, and pioneer of the Czech avant-garde, along with being a member of the resistance during the Second World War. He was a founder and leader of the influential artistic collective Devětsil. A Communist from 1921 until 1929 (when he was expelled from the party), he remained a leftist for the rest of his life. As a member of the Czech resistence under the Nazi occupation, Vančura headed the writers' section of the National Revolutionary Intelligence Committee. In 1942 he was executed by the SS in the reprisals for the assassination of Reinhard Heydrich. A highly influential author in his homeland, Vančura's creative work is influenced as much by Expressionism and his experiences in the First World War as by cinematography and the concept of Poetism, a movement he helped formulate with Devětsil; his writing spans the spectrum from social protest, such as *Baker Jan Marhoul* and *Ploughshares into Swords*, to poetic and humorous works like *Summer of Caprice* and the Czech children's classic *Kubula and Kuba Kubikula*. Humour is fundamental to Vančura's style, yet in each of his works it manifests itself differently, as subtle irony, parody, linguistic experimentation, and even "new methods of expression". Because of his extensive work in theatre and film, Vančura's literary works incorporate a number of dramatic and cinematic elements. This is perhaps one reason why his novels have been adapted so successfully for the screen. 1967 saw the release of two classic films based on Vančura's work: *Summer of Caprice*, directed by Jiří Menzel, is perhaps the most charming movie to come out of the Czechoslovak New Wave, while František Vláčil's version of *Markéta Lazarová*, Vančura's experimental and brutal historical novel, is the most critically acclaimed film in Czech cinema.

DAVID SHORT is the author of a popular Czech textbook, author or co-author of a number of publications in the field of linguistics, and a prolific translator from Czech and, to a lesser extent, Slovak. He spent 1966–72 in Prague, studying Czech and linguistics, working, translating, having fun, and eventually marrying a Czech student of Spanish at the same faculty. He then taught Czech and Slovak at the School of Slavonic and East European Studies in London from 1973 to 2011. He was awarded the Jiří Theiner Prize for his significant contribution to the dissemination and promotion of Czech literature abroad, the Czech Minister of Culture's Artis Bohemicae Amicis medal, and the Medal of Comenius University in Bratislava.

His translations include:
Vítězslav Nezval: *Valerie and her Week of Wonders*
Bohumil Hrabal: *Pirouettes on a Postage Stamp*
Karel Michal: *Everyday Spooks*
Jáchym Topol: *Gargling with Tar*
Karel Čapek: *Rossum's Universal Robots*
Daniela Hodrová: *Prague, I See a City...*
Jaroslav Durych: *God's Rainbow*
Bohumil Hrabal: *Rambling on: An Apprentice's Guide to the Gift of the Gab*
Bohumil Hrabal: *Why I Write?*
Róbert Gál: *Agnomia*

MODERN CZECH CLASSICS

Published titles

Zdeněk Jirotka: *Saturnin* (2003, 2005, 2009, 2013; pb 2016)

Vladislav Vančura: *Summer of Caprice* (2006; pb 2016)

Karel Poláček: *We Were a Handful* (2007; pb 2016)

Bohumil Hrabal: *Pirouettes on a Postage Stamp* (2008)

Karel Michal: *Everyday Spooks* (2008)

Eduard Bass: *The Chattertooth Eleven* (2009)

Jaroslav Hašek: *Behind the Lines: Bugulma and Other Stories* (2012; pb 2016)

Bohumil Hrabal: *Rambling On* (2014; pb 2016)

Ladislav Fuks: *Of Mice and Mooshaber* (2014)

Josef Jedlička: *Midway upon the Journey of Our Life* (2016)

Jaroslav Durych: *God's Rainbow* (2016)

Ladislav Fuks: *The Cremator* (2016)

Bohuslav Reynek: *The Well at Morning* (2017)

Viktor Dyk: *The Pied Piper* (2017)

Jiří R. Pick: *Society for the Prevention of Cruelty to Animals* (2018)

Views from the Inside: Czech Underground Literature and Culture (1948–1989), ed. M. Machovec (2018)

Ladislav Grosman: *The Shop on Main Street* (2019)

Bohumil Hrabal: *Why I Write? The Early Prose from 1945 to 1952* (2019)

Jiří Pelán: *Bohumil Hrabal: A Full-length Portrait* (2019)

Martin Machovec: *Writing Underground* (2019)

Ludvík Vaculík: *A Czech Dreambook* (2019)

Jaroslav Kvapil: *Rusalka* (2020)

Jiří Weil: *Lamentation for 77,297 Victims* (2021)

Forthcoming

Jan Procházka: *The Ear*

Ivan M. Jirous: *End of the World. Poetry and Prose*

Jan Čep: *Common Rue*

Jiří Weil: *Moscow – Border*

Jan Zábrana: *The Lesser Histories*

Libuše Moníková: *Verklärte Nacht*